LAST GUN
TO JERICHO

**Center Point
Large Print**

**This Large Print Book carries the
Seal of Approval of N.A.V.H.**

LAST GUN
TO JERICHO

JAMES KANE

CENTER POINT PUBLISHING
THORNDIKE, MAINE

This Center Point Large Print edition
is published in the year 2004 by arrangement with
Golden West Literary Agency.

The text of this Large Print edition is unabridged. In other
aspects, this book may vary from the original edition. Printed in
Thailand. Set in 16-point Times New Roman type.

ISBN 1-58547-505-X

Library of Congress Cataloging-in-Publication Data

Kane, James.
    Last gun to Jericho / James Kane.--Center Point large print ed.
      p. cm.
    ISBN 1-58547-505-X (lib. bdg. : alk. paper)
      1. Large type books. I. Title.

PS3505.O6646L375 2004
813'.6--dc22

                                                        2004008722

ONE

SHE'S IN JERICHO

I T WAS A DAY LIKE ANY OTHER DAY, AND JEFF CARTER came to town not expecting trouble.

He was a quiet man. Tall and lanky, he had the kind of body that burned energy fast. He was seldom seen wearing a gun. Yet there was something about him that indicated clearly that he was no stranger to guns.

Coming into town now behind a pair of high-spirited bay geldings, he looked like a country doctor— thoughtful, serious, dedicated. It was evident that he was well liked in Red Rock.

People on the street nodded to him, and hailed him: "Morning, Jeff. How're things on the ranch?" and he nodded back and smiled briefly. He was thirty years old, but he had the kind of flashing smile that took ten years from his face. At times like this he looked like a tow-haired boy with just a touch of devilry showing behind the gold-flecked gray of his eyes.

There was a time, however, when Jeff Carter had been known quite simply as 'Brazos' or 'that gambler from Texas'. He was the sort of man his friends would have gone through purgatory to defend; and his enemies through the same brimstone to kill.

Jeff had worked the river boats out of New Orleans, and the fact that he was still alive attested not only to his quite considerable skill with cards, but to his

7

equally proven ability with a gun.

But few people in Red Rock knew this of Jeff Carter. His banker knew, and so did Sheriff Tom Bates. The others knew him only as the man who had bought the Mack farm and turned it into a paying horse ranch.

For Jeff had always loved horses, and he seemed to like solitude. There was a reason.

It was close to noon of a bright sunny day when he pulled the buckboard to a stop in front of Olsen's General Store and went inside, checking a penciled list of supplies he had jotted down earlier.

Olsen was waiting on a farmer and his wife, and Jeff went around the near counter and picked out the few things he saw that he wanted. He was chewing tentatively on a hard soda cracker he had picked out of a barrel and waiting for Olsen to finish when the storekeeper asked: "You see him, Jeff?"

Jeff turned his attention to Olsen. The store owner was a balding man, quiet and efficient behind a counter, dour in conversation, excitable in a card game.

"See who?"

"Man who came looking for you."

Jeff put the cracker down on the counter, and a shadow passed briefly across his face. Instinctively, his right hand brushed down his weaponless hip and came away quickly, without being noticed by Olsen. But behind the calmness of his manner was a cold alertness.

He said: "No, I didn't see anyone."

8

Olsen finished with the farmer and his wife and motioned to a gangly boy to help carry the farmer's purchases out to his wagon. He came over to Jeff.

"Came in on the morning stage. Asked about you. Said he knew you lived around here."

Jeff didn't say anything.

Olsen looked a little worried. "I told him how to get to your place." He eyed Jeff. "He seemed to want to see you real bad."

Jeff nodded. "Well, thanks." He paid for his purchases.

"What shall I tell him when he comes back?"

Jeff considered this for a moment. "I'll be in town, probably in the sheriff's office."

He picked up his purchases and went outside and dumped them in the buckboard. Then he stood in the street and put his gaze on the road leading out of Red Rock.

It was a small town, out of the way of much travel. The stage stopped there only once a week.

It was years since anyone had come looking for him; he had begun to think the past was dead.

He crossed the street and went down the plank walk to the sheriff's office. Old Mose Bentham, part-time jailer, odd-time deputy, was scraping rust from a pair of handcuffs. Mose was generally tired, always irascible and, of course, unpredictable.

He looked up at Jeff, then down to his cuffs. He kept working.

Jeff asked: "Where's Tom?"

"Out."

9

Jeff waited in the doorway a bit. He knew Mose. When almost a minute passed without Mose volunteering anything further, he started to turn away.

Mose said without looking up: "Stranger came into town looking for you. Sheriff rode with him to your place."

Jeff waited patiently. He knew if Mose decided to say anything more, he'd take his time about it.

"Important-looking feller; looked like he owned the town." Mose turned to look up at Jeff now. "Mebbe a rich uncle, huh?"

Jeff was silent a moment, thinking back.

"Maybe," he said quietly, and went outside.

He stood on the walk outside the law office for a long time, studying the empty road out of town. The past crowded in on him.

He had buried himself in Red Rock seven years ago and had made himself a new life. He was reasonably content. There was even a girl in town, Mady Wilson, who was interested in him. But before he could really settle down there he had to get someone out of his mind—out of his life.

He stepped off the walk and started to cross towards his buckboard, and that was when he saw the buggy. It was coming down the road to town.

He waited, recognizing the thick, burly figure driving—Sheriff Bates. The man on the seat beside him, taller than the sheriff, had a familiar yet elusive silhouette.

They came rolling into town, and Sheriff Bates saw Jeff and swung the buggy in towards him.

"Must have missed you coming in," the sheriff grunted. He glanced at the man beside him.

"Hasn't changed much, has he?"

John Sturvesant smiled. He was a well-dressed, graying man with an easy smile. A solid gold watch chain caught the sun as it looped across his vest. He looked important—and he was.

"Hello, Jeff," he said.

Jeff nodded his greeting. "Long ride from Denver, Mr. Sturvesant?"

John smiled. "Not too long a ride to visit an old friend."

Jeff eyed him quizzically; there was a time when he and John Sturvesant had not been friends.

Tom Bates said heartily, "Well, I'll leave you two together." To John: "I'll drop the buggy off at the stables."

John nodded. "Thank you, Tom."

He stepped down beside Jeff. "Buy me a drink?"

Jeff nodded.

They walked down the street and turned into the Long Bar Saloon. It was small and quiet, and the sour smell of spilled beer tainted the air. The bartender was at the far end of the bar, setting up the quick lunch (free with beer) on the counter.

They found a table by the window, and Jeff said: "Beer?"

"Beer will be fine," John said, and took two cigars from his vest pocket. He extended one to Jeff.

Jeff took it and rolled it slowly between his fingers. Then he asked: "All right, John—what is it?"

11

John said: "A favor."

Jeff's eyes dropped, and he shook his head slightly. "I'm busy."

"Not too busy," John said. "Not according to Tom."

"The sheriff isn't keeping track of my time," Jeff said testily.

John grinned. "Don't be so touchy. I remember you when you were a laugh a minute."

Jeff eyed him soberly. "Sure. Now what do you want?"

"I want you to ride down to a town called Jericho, in New Mexico Territory, and find out something for me."

Jeff glanced at the bartender approaching them. "Two bottles of beer—on my tab." As the bartender went away, he turned to Sturvesant.

"Big John Sturvesant, boss of Wells Fargo, wants *me?*" He settled back in his chair and lighted up the cigar John had given him. "You could send a dozen of your own investigators—"

"I have," John interrupted, frowning.

Jeff waited.

"Two of them were killed. One disappeared."

Jeff didn't even consider it. He shook his head. "I'm sorry, John. I've retired."

"It would pay five thousand dollars," John said. "Now wait a minute," he cut Jeff off. "I know you can use the money; change that spread of yours from a one-horse ranch to something really going."

"*If* I got back," Jeff replied. His smile was a little crooked. "It's been a long time, John. I'm a little rusty."

"Not that rusty."

Jeff got to his feet. "Sorry, John," he repeated. "But it's still no deal."

He started to walk out.

John said: "Ten thousand dollars—and Dolores?"

Jeff turned. There was a tightness in his face now.

John nodded. "She's in Jericho."

Jeff walked back and sat down.

"You sure?"

"I'm sure."

Jeff said: "I gave up looking a long time ago." His eyes were shadowed. Then he shrugged. "All right, John—what do you want me to do in Jericho?"

John took a letter from his coat pocket and handed it across the table to Jeff. It was penned in a firm, clear hand.

Jeff scanned the letter. It read:

Dear John:

You owe me a letter, you calcified fossil. Ain't heard from you in way over six months. Only reason I'm writing now is because Bill wants his godfather at his wedding. Yep, the boy's getting hitched to the prettiest girl you ever laid eyes on: Ellen Bendore, daughter of my late partner, Henry. If you can unglue that butt of yours from your padded chair in Denver, come down and join in the celebration. We'll split a couple of bottles.

Frank Hayes.

Jeff handed the letter back, his eyes curious. "Frank Hayes?"

"My brother-in-law," John Sturvesant answered. He slipped the letter back into his pocket.

"This letter was written more than six months ago," John said quietly. "Three days after he mailed it, Frank Hayes disappeared with more than a quarter of a million in gold bullion. The bullion belonged to a mine owner in Jericho named Howard Pope. It was insured for the full face value by Wells Fargo."

Jeff frowned. "Frank Hayes ran off with a quarter of a million dollars in gold?"

John shrugged. "That's what Wells Fargo is being called upon to pay. But I'm not going to pay until I know for sure what happened to Frank. That's why I'm asking you to ride down to Jericho. I don't know what you'll find down there. But this much we do know. Frank Hayes rode shotgun on that last stage out of Jericho and didn't come back. His driver and the stage's only passenger, a whisky drummer, were found dead by the side of the road. But Frank and the stagecoach just vanished into thin air!"

He leaned back in his chair, his eyes shadowed, troubled. "The country was combed by a hundred men for almost a month. The law had been alerted from the Mexican to the Canadian borders. But no one's turned up information on Frank or the stage he was riding!"

Jeff was silent for a moment, remembering the country around Jericho. "He could have driven that stage into any one of a hundred desert canyons west of town," he pointed out, "and be taking it easy a thousand miles south of the Mexican border."

"Maybe," John Sturvesant agreed. "But I don't think so. He was my brother-in-law, but that isn't my reason. Why would a man who was looking forward to his son's wedding toss it all away? Frank wasn't hurting for money. The stage line was paying off. Why would Frank suddenly run out on his own son?"

Jeff shrugged.

He finished his beer. "You want me to find out what happened? That's all?"

John nodded. "If you do, it'll be more than anyone else has done."

Jeff stood up. "I'll leave in the morning."

John held out his hand. "Ten thousand dollars will be waiting for you, in your account, in the bank."

Jeff's smile was cold. "When I come back," he said. He walked out.

John sat at the table, looking after him.

TWO

TOPAH

In the morning Jeff made arrangements for Ellis Conway to look after his spread while he was away. Ellis, his wife, a crippled brother, and several growing children lived on the small ranch neighboring Jeff's place. Ellis could use the extra money.

"When will you be back?" Ellis wanted to know.

Jeff shrugged. "Before the snow flies." He waved to Ellis's wife and the two smaller Conways watching him from the doorway and rode away.

He had saddled the best horse on his spread, a big, fast palomino, and his slicker roll rode behind him. His cartridge belt and Frontier model six-gun were wrapped inside it—also a deck of cards. These were part of Jeff Carter's past.

He stopped by the Wilson farm on his way in to town. He couldn't leave without telling Mady Wilson.

Jock Wilson, Mad's father, was in the field, sharpening his plough. He nodded at Jeff's question. "She's in the barn."

There was bitterness in his voice. He watched Jeff ride away, and he thought wryly: *Can't ever trust a man with an itchy foot.* . . .

Mady was in the near stall, milking a tan-and-white cow. Even when she was seated on the stool you could see she was a tall girl—fair-haired, blue-eyed, snub-nosed. She was pretty, but there was no guile about her. She was twenty.

He stood in the doorway, watching her. The shadow of Dolores lay between him and this girl, and he couldn't shake it.

She sensed his presence finally and turned, and he said: "Hello, Mady. . . ."

She stood up quickly, facing him, her back against the stall boards. Her smile was small and tremulous on her full lips.

"Good morning, Jeff."

He took a deep breath. "I dropped by to say goodbye. I'm leaving Red Rock for a while."

She nodded. "I know. Father went to town last night; he heard you were leaving."

She worked hard to keep her voice from breaking. "I'm glad you stopped by to tell me."

He came to her then, his eyes searching her face, knowing he was hurting her, but unable to find the words to ease the pain.

"I have to go," he said. "I'm sorry. . . ."

A quick start of tears glistened in Mad's eyes. "Sorry. Now isn't that the most awful word Webster had to include in his dictionary?"

She turned then and ran out of the barn towards the house. Jeff stood watching her. For a moment he was tempted to go after her, tell her he would stay.

But for seven years the ghost of another woman had hung like an albatross around his neck. In Jericho he could finally lay that ghost to rest.

He walked to his waiting horse, mounted and rode away.

It was a long ride to Jericho. The country changed. The hills became bleak, jagged, dry and forbidding; the stretches between towns longer. Grass gave way to mesquite and catclaw; the wind that blew across the empty glaring valley had a thin and lonesome whine.

And Jeff Carter changed, like the land. He wore his six-gun on his hip now, and he drew and fired it countless times at targets that presented themselves—a running jack-rabbit, an odd-shaped stone, an occasional tin can discarded by an old camp site. Nights he practiced with the deck of cards, getting the stiffness out of his fingers, sharpening his perception.

And the old reckless glint began to reappear in his eyes as the past began to stir and live again inside him. He had buried himself in Red Rock too long. . . .

He was on the final leg of his journey, resting his horse, when an Indian boy appeared on the slope below him, moving like a puff of brown dust from behind the cover of a huge boulder. He was a slender youngster, wire hard and arrow straight, and he carried an old Henry carbine in his right hand.

The boy didn't see Jeff hunkered on the ledge above him, perhaps because he was so intent on something going on below him; something out of Jeff's narrowing, alert gaze.

Jeff's glance followed the boy. About ten years old, he judged. Crow probably, with some white blood in him. His black hair was long and tied on the nape of his slim neck with a piece of bright red calico. He wore a pair of ragged pants two sizes too big for him and nothing else.

A kid on the prowl for a rabbit? Or—?

Behind Jeff, his palomino moved restlessly, his whinny impatient. The youngster on the slope below Jeff whirled as though a rattler had struck at him. He jerked the old carbine around and fired in a quick, almost desperate movement.

Jeff had begun to move as the boy pivoted. The bullet chipped rock off the ledge where his boots had rested. Carter came down off the five-foot ledge, landing and sliding on a steep slope of loose dirt and gravel. He had drawn his gun, a reflex gesture, but he did not intend to use it. He had spotted the Henry as a singleshot, and he knew the youngster would not have time to reload before he got to him.

For a split-second, as he slid in the loose gravel and then regained his balance, he lost sight of the boy. When he looked again the youngster was gone, leaving a blurred image of a sun-bronzed torso sliding out of sight over the lip of a brush-choked arroyo, angling south from the hill.

Jeff pulled up, frowning. Ahead of him the rocky slope leveled off, then dipped again, hiding from his vision whatever the boy had been stalking. The afternoon heat shimmered with the fading echoes of the boy's shot.

It took Jeff less than a minute to reach the edge where the boy had paused. And then he saw what the youngster had been after.

The slope dropped steeply here to a small, brushy hollow. Two hundred yards below Jeff, four mounted men were wheeling away from a rude stone and rammed-earth shack. Four men—two sorrel horses, a black with a clipped tail and a big, mean-looking bay.

One of the riders brought up a Winchester as Jeff appeared on the rim above them. His aim was hasty, and the shot cut the air above Jeff, whining with a spiteful scream across the early afternoon sky.

Jeff held his fire. The range was too great for a Colt, and the bunched-up riders were not lingering for further hostilities. They were headed in a run towards the narrow trail that wound like a brown tape to the furnace flats below.

To the south of Jeff, at about his level, a Henry punched a bullet down to the fleeing riders. The slug rammed the rearmost rider, a burly-shouldered man, forward on his sorrel's neck. But he clung to his saddle, and in another moment they were out of range, diminishing rapidly in the heat haze.

The hills were silent again, holding only the echoes of that single carbine shot.

Jeff turned back to the ledge where he had picketed his horse. The palomino whinnied eagerly as he came up, loosening its tie reins.

Jeff paused. "Reckon we stumbled on to something we shouldn't have," he muttered. His voice held a cold neutrality. "Don't blame the kid for taking a shot at me, if what I guess happened took place."

He swung aboard the palomino, his glance ranging briefly to the vast sink below and past the last slope which he had been studying before the youngster with the Henry had come into his view. From here his angle of vision had cut him off from the shack in the hollow below, and his glance had been intent on the far scattering of buildings enclosed within the loop of a river which was dry eleven months of the year.

Jericho. An old mining town on the edge of— nothing. The Captains stood like stiff sentinels guarding the glaring white sands of the ancient sea bed—ragged, desolate peaks that faded into the high desert country of the Territory.

It didn't look like a town that was worth ten thousand dollars in anybody's market. But, according to John Sturvesant, a man and a stage carrying a quarter of a million dollars in gold bullion had disappeared from that town.

Jeff knew Jericho. In his old wild days, he had passed through the town on his way to the Mexican border. . . . He still found it hard to believe that this was where he would find Dolores. Crinoline and lace and the sweet smell of jasmine—these did not belong here. But John Sturvesant would not have lied to him.

Jeff took a deep breath and brought his thoughts back to immediate events. His gaze searched along the brush-choked arroyo where the Indian boy had vanished, and a tight frown made a line between his eyes.

"Take it easy, son," he muttered. "I'm neutral."

He let his horse find a way down the steep slopes. Ten minutes later he emerged into the hollow, rounding a stone corral where a half-dozen goats were grouped in a far corner, eyeing him with stupid belligerence.

The hut wall made up one wall of the corral. A small spring burbled in the stillness behind the shack. As Jeff pulled up to a halt, a rooster walked boldly out of the brush, stopping to eye him with cocked-headed pugnacity.

The riders, he now saw, had been more than visitors. The body sprawled across the threshold of the door, on the side away from his previous position on the slope, was that of a Crow Indian. He might have been forty, fifty, or older. He had a wrinkled leathery look that was old and yet ageless. His body was lean, bony, clad in a shapeless cotton shirt and worn corduroy pants.

Jeff knew the man was dead as he stepped over the body, disturbing the flies clustered around the blood-stained patch on the back of the man's shirt. The soft-nosed .45 slugs had ripped the life out of the man, coming out of his back. Jeff judged they must have been fired at close range.

The woman lay huddled in a far corner of the shack, as if she had tried to push her body as far away as possible from the ugly scene outside. The shack had no windows, and Jeff paused, letting his eyes grow accustomed to the light change. He did not see the woman right away, but he sensed her presence in the close room. And then she moaned, and he took three long strides towards her.

Jeff knelt beside her and knew instantly that she

was only a step or two ahead of death. She lifted her head slowly, staring with fierce hate, and then she must have understood he was not one of the men who had been there. The hate faded from her eyes.

"Topah," she breathed. "To-pah." The name faded, riding out on her last breath.

Jeff's head bowed. He could actually hear the stillness, it was so acute.

After a moment he rose, walked to the door and turned to look at the slope where the boy had disappeared. The sun was hot on his shoulders. But for the ticking of a second he felt a chill, as though a shadow had fallen across him. And in that moment he knew the boy's Henry was centered on him!

He didn't move. His glance ranged that rocky, desolate slope as though he were unaware of the scales being weighed in a boy's anguished mind. He saw nothing. Then the shadow lifted, and Jeff knew he had been spared.

The tightness in Jeff's shoulders eased. "Thanks, son," he muttered softly. "Reckon I'm in your way, anyway. I'll get the blazes out of here and let you do what you have to do."

He stepped away from the door, and now his glance picked up the glint of an object being studiously surveyed by the rooster. Humor glinted briefly in Jeff's eyes.

False teeth! An upper plate, evidently lost by one of the riders in his hurry to get away.

The rooster gave ground grudgingly as Jeff walked up, scooped the plate into his palm and dropped it into his pocket. He mounted and swung away, heading for the narrow trail leading down to the old lake bed and Jericho.

Up on the higher slopes, a pair of unwinking black eyes followed Jeff's progress—followed him until he was out of sight. The sun slid lower in the brassy sky, and the goats became restless and bleated for water. A few scrawny chickens, emboldened by the rooster's strutting, came out to peck in the hard-packed yard.

Stoically, the boy waited. When he was finally satisfied, he eased away from the mesquite clump where he had crouched, and on bare feet started down to the hut. There were no tears in his eyes, nor did his thin brown face show his loss or the loneliness that was making his insides an empty, aching hollow.

Somewhere, locked behind his dark and impassive gaze, hate began to chip loose; started filtering through the blood in his right arm until his fingers curled white against the scarred stock of the Henry.

The faces of the four men who had been there were burned indelibly into his brain.

THREE

GUN CHALLENGE

JERICHO LOOMED UP IN THE BRUTAL AFTERNOON heat—an old town as Territorial towns went. It had seen violent changes since its early beginnings as a Spanish outpost on the trail to Taos. It could remember when a Spanish *presidio* had guarded the ragged cluster of baked-mud huts squatting on the edge of the Sinks, which still retained a shallow lake of brackish water reflecting the unfriendly peaks of the Captains.

The lake had long since dried up, and the old Spanish name of Felicitas had given way to the biblical name of Jericho. The settlement had grown bigger and rowdier as gold strikes in the back hills had promised more than they actually produced. But on the strength of this false promise, Jericho had grown swiftly, given impetus by the tenuous projection of a railway spur that had never materialized.

In the fever of this speculative activity, Jericho had spread swiftly beyond the mud huts, lifting imposing structures above the ramshackle original dwellings. Optimistically, the boomers even laid out plats for a growth Jericho never achieved. Eventually the ocotillo and mesquite crept back over the plats, already drifted over with sand from the Sinks, and pack rats invaded the outermost, tenantless shacks.

25

By the time Jeff had first seen Jericho, the town had stabilized. The big TW and Anchor ranches, finding a new prosperity in rising beef prices and new silver strikes farther south, kept Jericho from dying altogether. And hard-eyed men, arriving along no known trails, found it safer to be west of the Pecos and less than a half-day's hard riding to the Mexican border.

He had been one of those men then, on his way to Mexico. . . . Now, eyeing the town ahead of him, Jeff wondered briefly if anyone in Jericho would remember him. Eight years was a long time.

The palomino's hoofs pounded over the worn planks spanning the dry river bed. Jeff turned left along the ineffectual moat, and his lidded glance lay briefly against the rising dust pall in the Sinks. The mud huts fronting the desert had a weather-honed, beaten look.

He turned right at Twin Springs Street, with the Sinks at his back now and the high-riding haze filtering the afternoon sun so that the trampled street dust had a reddish, smoky hue. Puffs of the dust lifted and whirled away under the palomino's reaching hoofs.

Twin Springs Street split Jericho in two. At the far end of the street it became a narrow road lifting up to the stamp mill on the hill. The mill's single stack showed no sign of activity.

Old recollections turned Jeff left again on Gold Street. And he saw that the Long Bar Stables were still in business. He wondered if Jake Sims, who had been scalped and left for dead by the Mescaleros ten years ago, still worked there.

And then, letting his gaze range along the dirty, unprepossessing buildings lining the streets, he still couldn't believe he would find Dolores living there.

A smallish, brown-faced, cold-eyed man shuffled out of the lean-to shack as Jeff pulled up in the stable yard and dismounted. Jake had not changed at all, Jeff saw. The long, ugly scar which ran from his right eye to the corner of his mouth gave his features a twisted and malevolent look. He still wore the same greasy hat over his scarred scalp.

Jake squinted at the tall man, and a frown came over his face. It worried him that he could not place this man.

"Another dust storm," he growled, shaking a bony fist unreasonably in the direction of the alkali Sinks. "Don't mind the sand so much," he added peevishly, "but it shore don't add spice to a man's grub." He peered at Jeff again, his eyes suspicious and unfriendly.

"You another one?"

"Another who?"

"Another danged insurance investigator!" The old man spat, and turned to run his hand over the big palomino's dust-caked flank. "Reckon you ain't," he answered himself, and explained it with his own brand of logic. "Never saw one of them Sherlocks have sense enough to own a hoss like this."

Jeff was untying his war bag. "You know what he

needs, Pop. Treat him right, use a gentle hand, and he'll give you no trouble."

Jake shrugged. He extended his left hand, palm up. "Not that I don't trust you, feller," he explained. "But way things are in town right now, you might not be around to pay me later."

Jeff grinned. He made a swift motion, plucked a five-dollar gold piece from under Jake's nose and dropped it into the man's hand.

The oldster snorted as he pocketed the money. "It'll take more than sleight of hand to get a man by in this town, stranger. I'll take care of yore cayuse—he looks smart. But if you got half as much sense as yore hoss, you'll keep moving. Jericho is on the edge of ripping wide open."

"Always did like a bit of excitement," Jeff murmured, picking up his duffel. "Helps pass away the time."

Jake's mouth tightened. He was trying to place this man with the smiling, likeable face—trying to remember when he had seen eyes like that before.

Jeff's voice interrupted his mental rummaging. "I'll step easy, old-timer. Just tell me where a gentleman can find a clean bed, and point out the liveliest place in town."

Jake's answer was that of a man who considers himself humoring a darn fool.

"The Tower House, biggest building in town, next to the Miners' Bank on Water Street. I ain't ever slept there—too fancy for my britches. The Comanche Bar will take yore money any way you want to part with it—over the bar or at the kind of game you think yo're lucky at."

He reached up to grasp the palomino's reins and then, not knowing why, added gruffly: "Let me give you a piece of warning, feller. If you find yoreself playing next to a jasper who looks like he's not old enough to wash behind his ears, has a narrow hoss face, straw hair an' freckles peppered across his nose, carries an old almanac in his hip pocket an'—wall," he paused for breath, "just make sure you deal yore cards from the top of the deck. An' don't try any of those fancy tricks you just pulled. You might find yoreself looking into the muzzle of a Colt just before it goes off."

Jeff's smile was quick and relaxed. "Why, Pop, thanks for the tip. I'll be sure to keep away from the Almanac Kid."

He picked up his war bag and moved away, a tall man with an easy, unhurried stride.

Jake watched him head for the corner of Jericho's Main Street. "It's yore funeral," he muttered. "You try that kid stuff against Quincey or the Faraday Kid, an' they'll eat you alive." He shook his head as he turned to lead Jeff's horse into the stable.

Moving along the walk, Jeff saw the dust storm begin to fan out like a ground-hugging fog off the Sinks as the wind began to rise. He quickened his step, wanting to check in at the hotel and wash the grit from his face and hands before the storm hit town. He had spent time in desert country, and he knew that a blow like this could last a few hours or could blow for days.

He turned the corner on Water Street and was halfway down the block when his glance picked up three horses huddled close together, nosing the rail across the street: a sorrel, a clipped-tail black and a big bay. Jeff's glance slid from the horses to the man lounging just to the side of the door of the building. He was watching the street like a man expecting someone. A small black cheroot dangled from his mouth. The sign over his head read: BALDY'S BAR & POOL.

Just ahead of Jeff, a girl stepped out of a doorway, carrying a loaded, linen-covered tray. He glimpsed her out of the corner of his eye, but he couldn't stop in time to avoid a collision. His shoulder rammed into the tray, and somebody's dinner went scattering across the plank walk.

The girl made an instinctive motion as if to pick up the irretrievable food, then straightened to face him, her cheeks flaming indignantly. "You—you—"

She was young and pretty, and despite the anger in her voice her blue eyes were close to tears.

"I deserve every bit of it," Jeff agreed, smiling sympathetically. "I should have been looking where I was going." He glanced down at the mess on the walk. "Allow me to buy you another dinner."

"Oh! It's not for me." The girl's voice was suddenly hurried. The color faded from her cheeks, her mouth trembled, and Jeff saw that her eyes were not on him but on someone behind him, in the street.

"Don't bother," she said quickly. "I'll get Joe to clean up. . . ."

A thin, high-pitched voice, which went with a boy who had not yet sprouted a beard, intruded. "I saw it, Ellen. I'll take care of it for you."

The girl called Ellen moved back, the color draining from her face. "No," she said. There was no strength in her voice. "I don't need—"

"No bother at all, Ellen—none at all!" The voice had a reedy chuckle to it.

Jeff turned, pinning an annoyed glance on the man just behind him, stepping up to the walk. He was looking for some gangly, pimple-faced kid, and a small shock of surprise went through him. Jake had described the man well. He didn't look a day over eighteen, but probably had lived a half-dozen more years. A tough, narrow-faced man, with freckles making a homely face even less likeable. Two crossed cartridge belts around a girl–small waist, pearl-handled Colts in tied-down holsters. A real badman— with a *Farmer's Almanac* sticking out of his hip pocket.

"Name's Quincey," the man said. He made it sound important. He leaned against the porch support less than six feet from Jeff and rubbed his slim back against it, like a lazy, stretching cat.

"You gonna pick up that stuff for the girl? Or do I have to rub your nose in it first?"

FOUR

THE HUMILIATION OF QUINCEY

Ellen's eyes flared with angry humiliation. She stepped between Jeff and the young killer, her chin jutting stubbornly.

"You keep out of this, Mr. Quincey!"

Quincey kept rubbing his back against the post. His yellow-flecked eyes had a cold, amused look.

"I ain't gonna hurt him, Miss Bendore," he disclaimed. His grin was like a cat's yawn, and as meaningless. "I just want to teach him manners."

The girl turned helplessly to the paunchy, middle-aged man who had come to the door of the lunchroom.

She said: "Mac—stop him!"

Quincey turned his gaze on the paunchy man. "Now, Mac," he said mildly, "you don't want to get yourself mixed up in this, do you?"

Mac shook his head and stepped back inside the lunch-room. Quincey turned to Jeff. "Well—?"

Jeff shrugged. "If that's all you want, mister—"

He bent to pick up a plate, but Quincey kicked it aside. "On your knees, feller. Pick it all up—on your knees!"

Jeff straightened slowly and eyed him. He had not wanted trouble, at least not until he had gotten his bearings there. But he saw now that talk wouldn't stop this man, nor would an apology. Quincey was obviously out to impress the girl in the only way he knew; he was going to show her how tough he was.

Irritation flickered in Jeff's eyes. Quincey's right hand was thumb-hooked in his cartridge belt; Jeff could see the "Q" carved into the pearl handle of his Colt.

"Maybe you'd better pick it up, then," he said coldly.

Ellen moved blindly between them again, determined to stop the killing she saw coming. Quincey brushed her back with a sweep of his left arm.

He was too close now, and nothing in Jeff's quiet face warned him. When Jeff moved, it was too late. Quincey's right hand jerked to his Colt, but Jeff's fingers closed over his knuckles like a steel band, pinning his hand against his holster as though clamped in a vice. At the same instant Jeff's right hand exploded against the gunman's mouth.

Quincey reeled back, tripping over Jeff's out-thrust leg. As he fell, he felt his Colt twisted out of his right hand as easily as though he were a child. Then he sprawled face down on the rough planking in front of the lunch-room.

With a savage energy he recoiled, pushing himself up. Jeff's boot came down hard between his shoulders, grinding his face into the boards. In the next instant Quincey felt his other Colt slipped from his holster.

Jeff stepped back, sent his gaze in a quick, alert appraisal of the immediate area. The walk had cleared abruptly at the first movement, and he had an uninterrupted view up and down the street. About ten yards away, a high-sided wagon had pulled in to the plank walk, and the driver jumped off the seat, scurrying across the road and out of the line of fire.

The girl had retreated to the lunch-room doorway; she was staring down at Quincey in stunned disbelief.

The gunman came to his feet in less of a hurry now and turned to face Jeff. Slowly he backed off until his shoulders touched the lunch-room wall. His face was drained white except for the blood on his lips and forming in bead-like globules on the long scratch on his nose. Across his nose and on his forehead the freckles stood out vividly, like brown polka dots.

Jeff hefted Quincey's fancy Colts in his hands. His own gun was still in his holster.

Something in Quincey's eyes told him this kid would never let this die; he decided to bring it to a head once and for all.

"Don't ever try to use these until you've grown big enough to handle them, son." Jeff's words were an insult, as he had intended them to be, and he saw Quincey shiver with impotent rage.

Contemptuously then, Jeff tossed one of the Colts to the tense, waiting killer.

Quincey lunged off the wall to meet it. His right hand plucked the glinting six-gun out of the air and he spun it around. He thumb-slipped the hammer as it settled into his palm. He fired just once—fired at a blurred shadow of a man who lunged aside an instant

34

before he let the hammer drop.

Smoke wreathed Jeff's hip, a racking explosion accompanying it. Quincey's right hand jerked back, and his Colt went spinning to the walk. He took one stunned, unbelieving look at his bleeding hand and then, crazy mad, jumped for the man who had outshot him.

Jeff holstered his gun in one fast movement and stepped forward. The sound of his fist against Quincey's jaw traveled a hundred yards along the breathless street. Quincey spun around and fell limply into the alley.

Jeff turned sharply, his back to the lunch-room, his hard glance ranging over the deserted street. Dust whorls raised their shimmering curtains and passed. Here and there heads popped into view, and then men began to emerge from doorways, converging cautiously towards the scene as though they were approaching a charge of dynamite.

The three men in front of the pool-hall had not moved. One of them gripped a cue stick. In the light of the fading day he was hard to define. But Jeff had the sudden tantalizing sense of having known this man—had a sudden hunch, too, that the man's upper lip sucked in over a toothless gum.

The driver of the wagon who had sought refuge in the pool-hall came across the street. He was climbing up to the seat when Jeff had a sudden reckless impulse. Taking a quick stride down into the alley, he bent over Quincey's unconscious figure and lifted him in one clean jerk to his shoulder. Five long steps took him to the tailgate of the wagon. As though he were handling a sack of oats, he dumped the kid into the back of the wagon.

The driver twisted on his seat, his eyes bulging. "Hey! I don't want to—"

"Where you headed?" Jeff's voice clipped him.

"Pottersville. Ten miles south of here."

"Dump him off at Pottersville," Jeff ordered. "He needs the night air."

The driver took a long look at Jeff's cold eyes, and all of a sudden he had trouble with his chaw of tobacco. Some of the juice trickled down his throat, and he gagged.

"Gee-up!" he cried, and the team lunged into their collars. Jeff waited on the walk until the wagon made a turn at the end of the street. Then his glance went to the three men bunched up in front of the pool-hall. The leather-faced man with the cue stick made a small motion with his shoulders and said something to the short, powerfully built man on his right. He and the man turned and went back inside the pool-room. The third man, younger and slighter of frame, ducked under the tie-bar, mounted the gray horse tied at the rail, and headed down the street in the opposite direction from that taken by the wagon.

Jeff turned to the girl. "I'll get you another tray, Miss," he said quietly. "It's the least I can do."

Ellen Bendore was looking down the street to the point where the wagon had disappeared.

"He'll be back!" she whispered tautly. "He'll kill you for what you've done to him!"

Jeff thought of the bone he felt give under his skinned knuckles.

"We'll worry about Quincey when he gets back," he said. He took her arm and led her back into the lunch-room. The few customers maintained an uneasy silence, concentrating with single-mindedness on their food.

The paunchy proprietor quickly prepared another tray, brushing aside the girl's faltering apology. "Don't worry, Ellen," he said quickly. "I'll have Juan clean up the mess outside."

Jeff had thrust Quincey's Colts inside his belt, his coat hiding them. He took the tray. "For your father, Miss Bendore?"

She seemed confused. She was worried, and the worry, Jeff sensed, was of long standing. It concerned itself with other matters than what had just happened.

"No," she said miserably. "It's for my fi—for the man I was to marry—"

Jeff frowned. "Is he hurt?"

She turned to him, seeking some shred of consolation in his voice. In the past months her life had come apart, and she no longer knew whom to trust. She had only Bill, but Bill desperately needed help, and time was growing short.

"No—no. He—" Her eyes held a bitter defiance as she turned to face the silent man in the lunch-room. "Bill's in jail."

Jeff sensed the stress in the girl. His smile was meant to ease her.

"Then he can stand a square meal," he said evenly.

He moved towards the door, feeling her reluctance to talk there. . . .

They walked down a narrow road flanked by windowless adobe buildings. This was an old part of town, the Spanish section fronting the old river bed and the Sinks, now haphazardly tenanted by a polyglot Indian-Mexican population.

They paused on the corner. Ellen eyed him, a small smile tugging at her mouth. "You're being very kind. But you don't have to do this for me." Her eyes darkened. "You're in trouble enough as it is—"

He shrugged. "That's why I came here, Miss Bendore. I'm Jeff Carter." He smiled. "I'm sure the name means little to you. But I came here to see if I could help you and Bill Hayes."

"Help Bill?" Ellen's eyes lighted with sudden hope. "Are you—from Wells Fargo?"

"In a way," Jeff said, "I am. No, I'm not a Wells Fargo investigator. But I happen to know John Sturvesant. He asked me to ride down here to try to find out what happened to Frank Hayes." He frowned. "John didn't know Frank's son was in jail."

Her fingers clutched at his arm. "I'm glad there is someone I can trust." Her lips trembled. "It's been so terrible since Bill's father vanished."

They started across the street.

"I'm afraid for Bill," Ellen continued. "The whole town has gone ugly since his father disappeared with the stage and a quarter of a million dollars in gold."

She sketched in what Jeff already knew of the robbery. "I don't know what to think about Bill's father," she confessed. "I'm confused. Frank Hayes was my father's partner. Tom Bendore and Frank started the Overland Stage Line together. My mother died when I was very young, and Dad raised me. Then, a year ago, my father came back from a trip with a wife. I didn't take to my stepmother too well. Dolores—Mrs. Bendore—was much younger than Dad—and very pretty. And—"

She looked up at Jeff as he stopped abruptly, facing her. "Dolores?" His voice was shallow, waiting. "Your stepmother's name is Dolores?"

Ellen nodded. "She was Dolores Camarillo before she married Father."

Jeff looked away, not wanting Ellen to see his face. After a moment he took a deep breath.

Ellen said, "Did you know her?"

"Yes," he answered. His voice was quiet now, and there was nothing to indicate the hurt inside him, the dying of a dream.

Ellen's eyes were troubled. "I don't mean to talk ill of her, Jeff. She's tried to be helpful to me since Father died shortly after he returned home with her. But Dolores has little knowledge of the stage line business—and I think she hates living here."

Jeff brought her back to her immediate problem. "Why was Bill jailed?"

Ellen shook her head. "On a fantastic charge by Howard Pope, owner of the High Life Mine. Pope claims that Bill must have helped his father plan the robbery. I think he called Bill an accessory—"

She seemed suddenly close to tears. "It's not true,

39

Jeff. Bill has worked for Mr. Chandler, in the bank, for years. He's not rough—not the sort of man who—" She fell silent, averting her face from Jeff's level regard.

They emerged on River Road, and the wind off the Sinks was gritty, stinging. Jeff's fingers tightened on the edges of the linen towel protecting the food on his tray.

The town marshal's office was located in a long, thick-walled structure which had been built as a strongpoint against Apache attacks. The heavy oak door was intended to withstand battering and the impact of arrows; its windows were narrow iron-grilled slots in the thick walls.

A big, burly-shouldered man with light-gray eyes peering down a thick hooked nose answered the girl's knock. He blocked the doorway, one hand holding a crumpled copy of the Police Gazette, the other holding a crumpled butt. His eyes went from the girl to Jeff. His careless appraisal turned suddenly intent, and a small frown made a crease above the bridge of his nose.

The nickel-plated badge on his dirty black shirt was scratched and hung lopsidedly, obviously an item about which he had little concern.

Ellen said meekly: "I want to see Bill. I've brought him something to eat."

The marshal tossed the copy of the Police Gazette on the desk behind him. "You're spoiling him," he sneered. His glance shifted to Jeff. "Who's the new boy friend?"

40

Ellen crimsoned. Jeff said easily. "A friend of the family, Marshal," and pushed his way past the scowling lawman.

He looked back at the marshal's barked command: "Just a minnit, feller! Put that tray down on the desk. Lay your gun belt down beside it!"

He stood scowling as Jeff obeyed. His eyes widened abruptly as Jeff placed Quincey's two guns alongside his gun belt.

"What are you," he demanded suspiciously, "a traveling arsenal?" He took a step closer to the desk and suddenly whirled, his gun sliding out of its holster.

"Those guns, mister! Where did you get them?"

Jeff shrugged. "Had a run-in with some young tough a few minutes ago," he answered drily. "Took his guns away from him so he wouldn't hurt himself."

Marshal Bart Hodges steadied himself against the battered filing cabinet. "You *what?*"

Ellen said: "Please, Mr. Hodges, I want to see Bill."

The marshal licked dry lips. "Yeah— sure." He took a large key ring from a hook above his desk. He looked at Jeff. "Where's that tough kid now, feller?"

"Last I saw of him," Jeff answered carelessly, "he was headed for Pottersville."

Bart Hodges sighed, a gusty exhalation. He walked to a door in the back wall and unlocked it. "Just the tray," he ordered shakily. "I'll give you both five minutes in there with him."

Frank Hayes' son was a wiry, tight-knit youngster with a thin, sensitive face roughened now by several days' growth of brown stubble. Despite Ellen's obvious solicitude, he looked as though he had eaten very little in the past week. His weary light-brown eyes indicated he had worn himself out during long sleepless nights in a mental search for understanding of what had happened.

Standing, he was not much taller than the girl who clung to him, her face on his shoulder, her voice small and sobbing.

"Bill—oh, Bill—"

He put his arms around her, his eyes on Jeff hard and questioning. Finally, he cupped a hand under Ellen's chin and lifted her face up to him. "You shouldn't keep coming here, Ellen." His voice sounded tired, beaten. "I'm not hungry, anyway."

"You must eat!" she said with the determined logic of a woman. "And Mr. Chandler said he was writing to the sheriff in Downey. They can't convict you on such flimsy charges—can they?"

She turned to Jeff, seeking reassurance from this tall, capable man.

"I'm not a lawyer, Miss Bendore," Jeff replied. "I couldn't say."

Bill Hayes made a motion to Jeff. "Who is he?" he asked Ellen.

Jeff answered for her, flashing Ellen a warning look. "A friend of Ellen's mother. . . ."

Bill reacted with displeasure to this. "Mrs. Bendore?" He looked at Ellen, who nodded. "And a friend of yours, too," she added quickly.

Bill sank back on his cot. "It's been one long night-

42

mare," he said bitterly. "All I keep thinking about is why Dad—what happened—"

The marshal's voice interrupted. "Time's up."

Ellen put a hand on Bill's head. He didn't look up. She hesitated; then her shoulders slumped and she turned to the door.

Out in the office, the marshal watched Jeff buckle on his gun belt. The lawman seemed puzzled, uncertain. And it occurred to Jeff that this man acted like a pawn. He was a man who took orders before carrying out a course of action. And obviously he had not yet received instructions as to how he should handle Jeff.

Jeff made a short motion towards Quincey's Colts. "You better keep them here, Marshal. The kid might want them when he comes back."

He took Ellen's arm and went outside before the lawman's dull brain fully absorbed this.

In the gritty dusk, Jeff walked the girl home. The Bendores lived in a neat frame house on a quiet side street. He paused at the gate, and she turned to him.

"You said you knew my stepmother. I think she's home—she'll be glad to see you."

Jeff hesitated, then shook his head. "Some other time." He wasn't ready to face Dolores—not yet. He was remembering the girl who had said she would wait for him when he got back—he had searched for her for five years.

And now he had found her—in Jericho—a married woman. John Sturvesant, he reflected bitterly, must have known.

Jeff had the sudden urge to ride out of Jericho that

very night, to wire John Sturvesant just where he could jam his ten thousand dollars.

Ellen's voice brought him back to the moment. She said: "Well, thank you for your help. I hope you can do something for Bill." Her voice trembled. "I'm afraid—"

He squeezed her arm gently. "Don't be," he said. "I don't think Bill is in any real danger. And no jury will convict a man on such circumstantial evidence."

"*If* Bill ever faces a jury!" she said bitterly. "I've been hearing ugly rumors all day, whispers of a lynching. The High Life miners spent a lot of money in town. Now the mine is closed down. It wouldn't be too hard to get some of the people stirred up, Jeff."

"They wouldn't go that far," Jeff said. "After all, the law—"

"Is at the county seat at Downey, seventy miles from here," Ellen pointed out. "Bart Hodges, the town marshal, was hired by Howard Pope, and he is paid by Pope. He would probably help them hang Bill."

Jeff's face was stiff. "Bill won't hang," he said quietly. "I promise you that, Ellen."

FIVE

THE BOSS OF HIGH LIFE

THE TOWN HOUSE HAD BEEN BUILT DURING JERICHO'S last boom period. It remained an anachronism in the midst of the settlement's squalid, jerry-built structures. Inside, its plush carpets had worn thin, and the mahogany wall paneling was scarred by careless boots. But it still retained an air of faded elegance, like an old man whose hopes are gone but who has not yet admitted this to himself.

Jeff Carter walked to the ornate desk, and the clerk, a neatly dressed man in his fifties, took off his gold-rimmed spectacles, wiped them on his spotless handkerchief and placed them carefully back on his nose. He peered at the tall man who approached the desk.

"Three dollars a day," he said in a voice querulously defiant, as though he were expecting an argument. "Week in advance."

Jeff made a pretence of going through his pockets. "Had some money," he muttered, and held back his laughter at the old man's stiffening attitude. "Why, heck," he said in mock surprise, "you got your hand on it, that's why." He put his palm over the old clerk's wrist and jerked the man's hand away, revealing to the clerk's startled gaze a twenty-dollar gold piece and a silver dollar.

Grave-faced, Jeff pulled the register towards him

and signed his name with a flourish.

"My room," Jeff said.

The clerk was still staring at the counter where his palm had rested; now he turned an icy gaze on Jeff. "We dislike parlor tricks in the Town House," he said haughtily. He banged his fist on the desk bell.

A bald Negro bellhop shuffled out of hiding from behind a potted palm and took Jeff's war bag. "Room twenty-one," the clerk said coldly, handing the porter Jeff's room key.

Jeff turned and followed the bellhop towards the broad, carpeted staircase in the middle of the lobby. Half-way up, they encount red a fat man heading down. Built like a fifty-gallon wine cask, the man was wearing an expensive gray suit, a dark-gray Derby hat and was clenching a fat unlighted cigar between his teeth.

He was in Jeff's way, and he paused, his small eyes, hard and slate-gray and expressionless, making a quick appraisal. A gleam flickered across them, and the cigar tilted slackly for a moment; then his teeth bit hard on it, and a fatuous look spread across his moon face.

"Gosh!" he exclaimed. "I'm getting so's I take up too much room, mister. Sorry." He smiled apologetically and stepped to the left, crowding the banister, and sidled past them down into the lobby.

Jeff glanced back. The fat man walked to the desk and said something to the clerk, who turned to look into the bank of pigeonholes. While the clerk's back was turned, the fat man looked down at the open register, then turned to look at the stairs. He saw Jeff watching, and he made a brief, strange gesture before the clerk, turning, took his attention.

Jeff turned to follow the bellhop, who was waiting for him at the landing. There was little about the fat man to jog Jeff's memory, and yet something nagged at a corner of his mind, and he tried to grasp it.

He asked the Negro porter, and the bald head nodded vigorously. "Mister Pringle? Yessir. Cigar salesman. Been here almost two weeks. Real nice gentleman, sir."

The porter paused a third of the way down the hallway, fitted the key into the lock and swung the door wide. He walked up to the bed, placed Jeff's bag on a stool and opened the window. It looked down on the veranda which ran across the front of the hotel and along sides of the big building, terminating in a long flight of stairs leading to the back yard.

A gust of wind drifted fine sand into the room, and the porter cracked the window down to a mere two-inch opening, shaking his head. "Mighty poor weather we been having, sir. . . ."

Jeff gave him a quarter.

"Thank you, boss. Anythin' else?" he asked, showing white teeth in a suggestive grin.

"A deck of cards," Jeff answered. He added a dollar to the quarter, and had washed and was about to start shaving when the porter reappeared with the sealed deck.

Jeff finished shaving and changed into a clean white shirt and black string tie. He glanced into the

47

smoky mirror, and the man he saw was a reflection of the old Jeff Carter, river-boat gambler; a little older, a little less reckless.

He put his right hand on the dresser top, palm down. At the mental count of three, his hand disappeared and reappeared with a Colt cocked and aimed at his reflection. He smiled crookedly as he slid his gun back into its holster. He had lost little of his old ability with a Colt. How much had he lost of his skill with a deck of cards?

Seating himself at the small table, he broke the seal and riffled the new cards. It had been a long time since he had played against professionals. Now he worked the stiffness out of his long fingers, shuffling and dealing. There were few men who could sneak a bottom card without Jeff knowing, and he was a past master at draw poker.

After more than an hour of this, he discarded the deck, dusted his coat and hat and went down into the lobby to have his boots shined. The sound of clinking dishes from the dining-room attracted him, and he went through the archway, ready to face whatever the night had to offer.

Jeff was mid-way through his evening meal when two men paused in the lobby doorway and looked over the diners. He was facing them, and he saw their gaze rest on him; then they came on into the dining-room, cutting among the tables to him.

The slighter, shorter man was expensively dressed, almost nattily so. His gray doeskin trousers were sharply creased, his expensive boots highly polished. Across his plum-colored waistcoat a loop of heavy gold chain glinted in the lamplight.

But under this expensive finery was a tortured shell of a man. His right arm hung limp at his side, and the gray glove hid but did not entirely disguise his mutilated hand. His pearl-gray hat covered a sparse growth of snow-white hair. His narrow face was badly scarred by fire; Jeff had the feeling that burning brands had, at some time in the past, been held against his cheeks. Deep lines scared his forehead, and his mouth was a bitter warp, permanently impressed.

The man with him was taller by at least six inches. He was probably as tall as Jeff, not so wide of shoulder, but lean and fit-looking. He was neatly dressed in a blue suit only slightly darker than his eyes, which appraised Jeff with cool restraint. He was in his thirties, Jeff judged. A hard, careful man—a handsome man made conspicuously so by contrast with his companion.

But as they made their way to the table, Jeff knew at once who had the authority by the way the tall man hung back slightly in deference to the scarred man.

They stopped by Jeff's table, and the shorter man dropped his hat on a cleared spot on the table, pulled out a chair and sat down. The tall man stood behind him, his fingers plucking a cigar from his breast pocket.

"I'm Howard Pope," the scarred man said abruptly. "You looking for me?"

Jeff glanced at him over the rim of his coffee cup. "No."

Above the scar tissue, Pope's eyes were as dark as wet plate. "You've heard of me?" he insisted. His voice held a shrill arrogance.

Jeff shrugged.

The tall man had his cigar going; he dropped into the chair beside his companion and interjected himself into the conversation.

"You came to town less than three hours ago!" he snapped. "In that short space of time you have trouble with Quincey, you get friendly with Ellen Bendore, and you visit Bill Hayes in jail." His cold glance was measuring Jeff, trying to place him. "In view of what's happened in this town," he added curtly, "Mr. Pope and I would like to know who you are!"

"The name's on the hotel register," Jeff said.

"Any name can be signed in that register!" the man snapped. "We want to know why you came to Jericho!"

Jeff sighed. He placed a deck of cards on the table, cut, and turned up an ace of spades. He replaced the cut, drew his empty hand back from the deck, then leaned forward and plucked the ace of spades from behind Pope's ear. He dropped it casually on the table.

"Cards are my business, gentlemen." His smile was guileless. "No overhead, very little equipment, and, as the prophet said, little profit."

The tall man's eyes had a dangerous glitter. "Not many gamblers could handle Quincey the way you did, Mr.—"

"Sharp," Jeff supplied smoothly. "Mine is a much misunderstood profession," he answered coolly. "A man has to learn to protect himself in my business."

"I don't give a hoot what your business is!" Pope snarled. He hadn't been pleased with the verbal fencing between Jeff and his companion, and he said so. "Connors, you keep out of this!"

He turned to Jeff, his voice ugly.

"The Hayes family aren't liked in this town, Sharp! Not since Frank Hayes disappeared with a quarter of a million dollars in gold bullion. Gold that came from my mine, the High Life!"

He took a dragging breath, a flicker of insane hate glinting in the muddy depths of his eyes. "The High Life was the only producing mine in the vicinity. I've had to stop production until I get a Wells Fargo check covering my loss. I'm telling you this so you'll know why anyone associated with the Hayes family isn't welcome here."

Jeff nodded. "Makes sense," he agreed. "Happens that I never met Bill Hayes or his father, either," he said truthfully. "I ran into Miss Bendore on the street, knocked a tray out of her hands by accident. It might have ended there," he continued, "if this Quincey kid hadn't tried to impress the girl with his toughness." He shrugged. "Least I could do after the accident was to carry Miss Bendore's tray for her."

Pope shoved his chair back and stood up. "We understand each other, then, Sharp. Stick to cards, and we won't have any trouble."

A small smile played across Jeff's lips as he

51

watched them depart. He had been expecting a kick-back from the afternoon's events, and he was only mildly surprised to have it come from the High Life owner.

Almost a hundred men had scoured the country after Frank Hayes' disappearance, Sturvesant had said, without finding a trace of the man, the stage, and the fortune in gold bullion. It stood to reason that Frank could not have left the Sinks. Assuming that Frank was innocent, then someone was playing for big stakes and knew what had happened to Frank and the bullion. Whoever that was would have reason to play up Frank Hayes' guilt. But why bring in his son Bill?

Something in Howard Pope's glittering eyes came back to annoy Jeff—a nameless bitter hatred in his voice as Pope had mentioned Frank Hayes; a hatred that seemed to be rooted deeper than the loss of the mine's gold bullion, although a quarter of a million dollars, Jeff reasoned soberly, would be enough for many men.

He finished his supper and lighted a cigarette. He had managed to convince Pope and his man Connors that he was what he claimed to be, an itinerant gambler handy with a gun, which, he reflected wryly, was not too far from the truth. His anger with John Sturvesant had diminished. Dolores had been the main reason he had come to Jericho, but John's promise of ten thousand dollars was his reason for staying.

In the meantime, he'd let things come as they might. Rising, he left a tip with money for his bill and went outside. The sky was dark and lamplight splotched the street, cutting dimly through the swirls of sand. Grit stung his face.

With a rising, muttering wind off the Sinks, the street was all but deserted. Jeff flicked his butt into the dust and recalled Jake's suggestion that the Comanche Bar was a likely place to lose his money.

Pulling his hat brim over his eyes, the tall man headed up the street. He walked two blocks before slowing down, his glance probing for sign of the bar.

The Overland Stage office lay directly across the street, its windows glowing yellow, and he wondered if it was still operating. He stiffened slightly as he saw a figure outlined briefly in the lamplight on the walk.

A small, wiry, half-naked boy was carrying a rifle! He was gone almost immediately, merging into the blankness of an alley between the stage office and the next building.

But the brief glimpse had brought Jeff Carter's thoughts back to a hot box canyon, to a crumpled Indian lying face down in front of a stone shack, and a woman's dying breath. . . .

Topah had come to Jericho!

SIX

WARNING FROM POPE

LIKE THE TOWER HOUSE, THE COMANCHE BAR WAS out of place in the desert town. It was big, with an air of elegance at odds with its rough-garbed customers. Red curtains shrouded the windows, and a half-dozen chandelier oil lamps, festooned with polished glass, lighted up the place.

Jeff made his way to the polished cherrywood bar, ordered whisky, and let it stand at his elbow as he turned to survey the crowd. Howard Pope and his man, Connors, were in a poker game at a near-by table. Pope's scarred face was turned towards him; the man nodded briefly and made a motion for Jeff to join them.

About to accept, Jeff felt a hand on his arm. "Let me buy you a drink, friend?"

He turned to look into Pringle's fat, sweat-filmed face. The cigar salesman mopped his brow with a handkerchief. "Sorry about getting in your way at the hotel," he apologized again.

Jeff shrugged. The man seemed intent on talking with him. His words kept tumbling out as he mopped his face. "Been here two weeks. Didn't get to sell many cigars, but"—his voice lowered as though he were running out of breath—"I learned a few things—"

Jeff said shortly: "I bet you did." He pulled away, his voice blunt. "Excuse me, feller. I think I'll sit in a poker game."

Disappointment flitted across the fat man's face. But he merely said, "Oh, sure, don't mind me. Get kind of lonesome, though, sometimes. Here," he said as Jeff started to walk away. "Have a cigar." He was fumbling in his vest pocket, thumbing through half a dozen smokes. "Compliments of my company."

Jeff took the cigar and thrust it into his shirt pocket. "Thanks. I'll smoke it later."

Howard Pope kicked a chair out for him as he approached the poker table, and Jeff dropped into it. Pope said, "You know my mine superintendent, Frank Connors." He motioned to the other man at the table. "Mr. Sharp—meet Tim Bolton, foreman of the TW spread, south of here."

Bolton, a raw-boned man of forty with a sandy moustache, nodded in greeting. Pope added thinly: "Watch out for Mr. Sharp, Tim—he does tricks with cards."

Bolton was eyeing Jeff with careful appraisal. "Saw him do tricks with a gun, too," he said noncommittally. He addressed himself to Pope. "Quincey show up yet?"

Pope scowled. "Haven't seen him." He looked at Jeff. "Quincey worked for me—sort of helped Connors here look after things at the mine. I'll tell him to lay off when he comes back."

Jeff breathed an audible sigh of relief. "I'll buy the next round, just to show my appreciation, Mr. Pope. I sure didn't want to start off on the wrong foot my first day in town."

They played for about a half-hour, at which time Jeff was ahead about ten dollars. A few people drifted in, but Jeff suspected the weather was against a full house tonight.

It was eight-thirty when a spare, gray-templed man in conservative dark clothes entered the Comanche Bar. He paused briefly inside the door, made a swift search of the room, and then came directly towards Jeff's table.

Pope noticed him before the man was half-way across the room. The mine owner shot a quick, meaningful look at Connors. Connors' lips twitched, and a sour look came into his eyes.

"Thought I'd find you in here, Howard!" the newcomer said sharply.

"Pull up a chair, Calvin," Pope said. "We promise not to win too much of the bank's money from you."

"The devil with poker tonight!" the man snapped. Close up and under the lamplight, Jeff saw that this man was older than he had first appeared—the lines were deep-etched around his eyes and mouth.

"There's a boy about to be lynched!" the man went on angrily. "An innocent boy, Howard! And you talk of poker!"

Pope leaned back in his chair, his face made more hideous by his sudden anger. "I think you're letting your imagination get the better of you, Calvin!" he said harshly. "And anyway, I don't agree with you that Bill Hayes is innocent!"

Calvin Chandler stiffened. He measured his bitter reply so that each word fell like a sharp pebble against rock.

"Howard—there's a mob in the Nugget Bar right now. Most of them are drunk—on free liquor. I don't know who's paying for the whisky. But I do know that two of your men, Whitey Smith and Tol Oliver, are doing most of the talking. *Your men, Howard!*"

Pope shrugged. He turned and crooked a finger to the watching bartender. "Sit down, Calvin," he said. "You need a drink."

The banker's face went white. "If that boy is lynched, Howard, so help me, it'll be on your head—"

"The devil with young Hayes!" Pope burst in harshly. "I don't think the boys intend to take the law into their hands. But if they do, they'll be doing this town a favor. I lost a quarter of a million dollars to his old man—but the town lost a lot, too, when I had to shut down. Hang it all, Calvin, I wouldn't raise a finger to help any Hayes!"

Calvin Chandler turned, his eyes searching among the scattered men in the bar. His voice rang with thin desperation. "I don't care what Frank Hayes did. I've been in this town a long time. It's got a bad name now. But if that boy hangs because of what Frank Hayes is *supposed* to have done, Jericho will never live it down! And I'll personally see to it that every man responsible, any man who takes a hand in it, is brought to justice!"

An uneasy silence followed his outburst. Pope's

eyes had a crazy, expectant glitter. No one moved, no one said anything.

Chandler's shoulders sagged. He walked across the room and went out without looking back.

Bolton grinned uneasily. "Last time we strung a man up was three years ago. Me an' some of the boys ran him down in the rough country under Cheyenne Peak. You know," he added, trying to erase the tension around the table, "the darn fool had the nerve to tell us he was only trying to help us out. Claimed he was herding our beef the long way around to our range. Why, we was almost sorry to hang the cuss—"

Connors laughed shortly, and Pope sneered. "No more of this lynching talk, Tim. I want a chance to win my ten dollars back." He looked at Jeff. "If I don't get that check from Wells Fargo soon, I'll have to start borrowing money to live on."

They played several more hands, and Jeff managed to lose thirty dollars. He slammed his cards into the discards and shoved his chair back. "That cleans me out temporarily, boys. If you'll stay around awhile, I'll be back, soon as I lay my hands on the rest of my bankroll I left in my room."

Connors reached out, pushing chips towards Jeff. "I'll loan you fifty—"

"I never play poker with anyone else's money," Jeff refused. "Bad luck." He nodded shortly, paused to finish his drink, and left.

The abrasive wind stung his face as he paused on the corner. The Nugget Bar was on Twin Springs Street, a block and a half away. From that direction the wind brought the sound of voices. Shouts rode the angry wind.

Jeff stepped into the sandy street and ran silently back to the hotel. He made a leisurely entrance, paused at the desk to check the time and to make sure the clerk would remember he had come in. He went up to his room, crossed to the window and climbed out to the veranda.

Several shots, punctuated by drunken yells, drifted to him as he headed for the back stairs. If he wanted to save Bill Hayes' neck, he would have to work fast!

SEVEN

DOLORES

MARSHAL HODGES WAS NERVOUS. HE PACED INSIDE his big, littered office, eyeing the battered alarm clock on his desk every fifth turn he made around the room. Inside the law office, only his pacing broke the stillness. Outside, driven particles of sand scampered like a swarm of mice across the heavy door and the narrow-framed windows.

He wanted a drink badly, but he knew he would have to wait until it was over—until they had come for the kid. He had to make it look right.

He stopped by the desk and took down the cell keys and dropped them beside the alarm clock where they would be easy to find. It would have to be done fast, before any of the drunken fools had a chance to realize what they were doing.

He was just about to sink into a chair when a fist pounded on the locked door. He lurched up, his face tightening. Palming his Colt, he went to the door, started to open it; then caution held his hand.

"Who is it?" he growled.

"Tol Oliver!" the muffled voice replied. "Open up! They're coming for the Hayes boy—"

Bart dropped his Colt back into its holster and snicked the heavy bolt back. He had not been informed that Oliver would be in ahead of the mob.

60

He started to yank the door open, his voice edged with impatience. "Hang it all, Tol—"

The shoulder ramming against the other side of the door sent it crashing into him, sent him stumbling backwards, stars pinwheeling before his eyes. He caught a blurred glimpse of a tall, broad-shouldered man moving towards him, and he made a spasmodic grab for his Colt.

Jeff's iron fist scraped the marshal's belt buckle as it drove into the lawman's stomach. The impact whooshed the breath out of the big man, jack-knifing him. Jeff wasted no time. His right knee came up into Bart's face, mashing his nose, loosening teeth. The lawman flipped backwards and landed heavily on the back of his shoulders.

Carter didn't give him another glance. He barred the door, scooped up the cell keys and ran for the rear door.

Bill Hayes was sitting on his bunk, a dull resigned expression in his eyes. He looked up at Jeff as the ex-gambler entered his cell.

"We've got two minutes to clear out of here!" Jeff snapped. "Get your hat!"

Bill stared. He didn't move, and Jeff uttered an impatient growl. He strode to the youngster, yanked him roughly to his feet and shoved him towards the cell door.

"I promised Ellen nothing would happen to you," he muttered. "Come on."

But Bill balked in the office. He looked down at the marshal's bloody face, then up at Jeff, and he started to back away.

"No! I don't know who you are, mister! Why should you help me?" His jaw jutted suspiciously. "It might be a trick to make me break the law so that—"

"Right now there isn't any law to speak of in Jericho," Jeff cut in harshly. "Until there is, I'm as much law as you'll need!"

Bill looked down at the unconscious marshal, then back to Jeff. His jaw was tight. "Just who are you, mister?"

Jeff mentally cursed the delay Bill's stubbornness was causing.

"A friend of John Sturvesant," he snapped. "I was sent down to find out what happened to your father!"

"Then you're a Wells Fargo man?"

Jeff didn't take the time to deny it. "Kid—there's a mob heading this way. One of them will be carrying a rope. We'll palaver later."

He was bending over the unconscious Hodges as he talked. His shoulder muscles bunched, strained against his coat as he hauled the man up and got his right shoulder under Bart's middle.

"Open up and let's get out of here!"

Bill flung open the door, and they went out into the night. Hayes closed the door behind him and followed Jeff across the street to the drop-off into the dry river bed. They slid down the sandy bank together, and the man from Red Rock turned sharply towards a dark clump of mesquite twenty feet down the arroyo.

A saddled horse snorted at their approach and jerked at reins knotted around a slender branch.

"His owner's going to raise a howl when he staggers out of the Last Call Saloon," Jeff said grimly. "Serves him right for leaving his cayuse tied to the rack on a night like this."

Bill hesitated. "Where are we going?"

"Not we," Jeff corrected him. "You—and him!" He was working swiftly, using the lariat coiled on the bay's saddle to tie the marshal securely.

"I want you to get him out of town, anywhere. But keep him with you."

"Out of town? Where?"

Jeff thought fast. "Ran across an Indian shack in the hills, south of here. In a box canyon—"

"Old Pete's place," Bill broke in. "Sure. Pete's an old friend of the family—"

"Was," Jeff cut in grimly. "Pete's dead." He didn't elaborate. "I think his boy's in town, probably looking for the men who killed his father and mother. You'll be alone up there. Stay put until I come for you."

Bill started to protest. Jeff cut him short. "Get moving. I've got to get back to town."

"What about Ellen?" Bill's voice was desperate. "She'll think that I—"

Jeff slapped the animal's rump. "I'll tell her," he promised as the bay lunged forward. He watched the burdened horse move away down the arroyo. . . .

Sand filtered down over him as the wind riffled along the banks. In the distance, a babel of voices and shots moving towards the marshal's office brought a thin smile to his face.

He doubted if, in the confusion when they found no one in the law office, the mob would think of

63

searching for tracks in the arroyo. And by morning all traces of Bill's flight would be gone.

Jeff Carter kept to the dry river bed, running swiftly in the night. Fifteen minutes later he came up behind the dark square bulk of the hotel and started up the long back flight of stairs. He walked quietly, breathing easily.

As silent as a cat, he stalked along the second-floor veranda. Of the windows facing the balcony, only one was lighted. He passed this without being seen or heard.

His own window was dark, as he had left it. He raised the sash carefully, thrust a long leg across the sill and ducked his head inside.

From the darkness within, a small-caliber gun made a sharp barking sound! The bullet punched a hole in the window three inches above Jeff's head!

Jeff's motions were instinctive. He was already more inside the room than out—he kept moving in. Bedsprings creaked thinly as a body stood up. The intruder started to run for the door.

Metal glinted in some stray source of light from the open window. Jeff lunged for the vaguely seen shape, caught up with the intruder at the door and cuffed at the glinting object. He felt his palm slap against a gun, heard it slide across the floor. Then his arm went around the prowler's body, shifted upward, and a grunt of surprise escaped him.

The bulging softness under his forearm belonged to no man!

The figure squirmed in his grasp, and he felt soft, silky hair brush his face—a tantalizing scent of lilacs tingled in his nose. The squirming figure suddenly quit struggling, lay quiescent in the curve of his arm, and a soft voice sighed, "Jeff—it's you?"

Jeff checked the quick shock of surprise. The soft, throaty voice rang a faint bell of memory in his head. He was placing the familiar scent of lilacs, the voice that could still send a tingle of anticipation through him.

"Jeff Carter!" the voice sighed softly. "Don't you remember me?"

He dropped his arms and moved away from her, and her voice followed him, chiding: "Jeff—you don't remember! And yet you said you'd never forget—"

He struck a match, turned to the oil lamp on the table by the dresser and tilted the glass chimney. In the red flare, his face had a dark, stormy look. The wick caught, and he set the glass chimney and turned to face Dolores Bendore!

She was sitting on the edge of the bed now, the skirt of her dress pulled up to reveal a shapely pair of ankles. A slender woman, taller than average, with a fullness of figure her high-necked dress couldn't conceal. A strikingly handsome woman who would have caused heads to turn at any social function. And it occurred to Jeff bitterly in that moment that he was still in love with her.

She looked at him, knowing this with intuitive wisdom. Her dark eyes teased him. "Do you always come into your room through the window, Jeff?"

"Only when I have visitors who wait in the dark with guns in their hands," he answered stiffly. He walked to the window, closed it, and drew the cracked shade down to the sill.

The woman pouted, her full red lips and eyes roguishly inviting. "I wanted to surprise you," she said.

Jeff looked at her, his eyes dark and tortured. "You have. . . ."

"But not this way," she added quickly. "When I heard someone at the window, I got frightened."

Jeff moved back, picked up the nickel-plated pistol which lay against the baseboard, and tossed it on the bed beside her handbag.

"Jeff—you're angry?"

His voice had an edge. "Surprised; not angry. I didn't expect to find Dolores"—he paused, his voice going deliberately cold—"I mean Mrs. Bendore, in a place like Jericho."

"Jeff—"

He over-rode her, his voice savage, taunting. "Not Dolores Camarilla, the toast of New Orleans. Expensive, perfumed Dolores—"

She got up and put her arms around him. "You are hurt, aren't you, Jeff?"

He wanted to pull away, but he couldn't. He had searched for this woman too long, wanted her too much.

"I waited," she breathed. "But you—you didn't come back. . . ."

"I told you a year. . . ."

66

"Six months too long." Her voice was low, sad—she turned away from him. "Something happened—I had to go away."

"I heard about young Raoul," Jeff said coldly. "They said he killed himself because of you."

She shrugged. "His family made New Orleans unpleasant for me. I couldn't stay. . . ."

"Where did you go?"

"It doesn't matter, does it?" She stood in the shadows, a tall, still magnificent woman. "I don't even want to remember."

"I searched two years for you," Jeff said. "I never stopped thinking about you."

She was silent for a moment. Then, "I wish you had found me. . . ." Her voice was sad. "I wish you had found me, Jeff. . . ."

She came to him. "I met Tom Bendore three years ago, in Houston. I knew he had a business of some kind back here in Jericho, a place I had never heard of. He was very attentive and flattering, and he made it all sound very interesting, and I guess I was tired of traveling."

She sighed. Her lilac scent seemed to fill the room, and all the old memories came alive in Jeff Carter.

"Anyway, here I am. Tom, unfortunately, died last year, and I—well, I found myself part-owner of a stage line and not much else."

Jeff frowned. "Why did you come here tonight?"

"I was in the stage office when I saw you go by. You went into the Comanche Bar, I think. I have few friends here and, when I saw you, it was a shock,

Jeff. I just couldn't believe it. I wanted to run out to you."

"Why didn't you?"

The emotion in her voice faded, and she sounded tired. "Don't punish me. Not now. . . ."

The barriers of bitterness broke down in Jeff, and he moved to her and took her into his arms.

"I'm sorry," he said quietly.

"Life gets so mixed up." She snuggled up against him, resting her cheek against his chest. "I should have waited for you, Jeff."

He held her close, thinking that this was what he had wanted through the years. Yet something was different; something was wrong. It was not that she had married and was now a widow. No, it was something else—something he couldn't quite define, a change within himself. What had once seemed glamorous and desirable had lost its edge. Perhaps he had waited too long.

Dolores broke into his thoughts. "Why did you come to Jericho?"

"For you."

She looked up, her eyes searching his face. "In this God-forsaken place? How did you know?"

"John Sturvesant told me," he answered shortly.

"Sturvesant? Who is he?"

"Regional boss of Wells Fargo. I knew him once—owed him a favor."

She pulled away from him, a small hurt smile on her lips. "Then you really didn't come here for me. You're working for Wells Fargo!"

He shrugged. "It was the price I paid for finding out you were here."

She sat down on the bed and slipped her pistol into her handbag.

"I understand," she said. "I have no right—" Her eyes were fixed on Jeff's face. "You came to find out about Frank Hayes, didn't you? About the gold he stole?"

"*If* he stole it!"

Her eyes darkened, and a wry smile momentarily added hard years to her face. "He stole it, Jeff—*I'm* sure of it! And I haven't stopped hating him for it!"

He came close to her, remembering Ellen Bendore's frightened face, young Bill's dazed features—two young people who didn't know how or why such a thing had happened to them. And he remembered sharply, too, John Sturvesant's conviction that Frank Hayes could not have stolen that bullion. . . .

"I didn't know Frank Hayes," he said. "But John Sturvesant did."

"And he doesn't believe Frank stole the gold shipment?" Dolores reached out and pulled Jeff down on the bed beside her. "I'm telling you why I know, Jeff. I want you to believe me."

Jeff waited. A small part of him remained suspicious, kept nagging at him with a question he could not put aside. Why had Dolores come to his room tonight, like a woman keeping a tryst? There had been no need. She could have sent for him in the morning.

"You must believe me," Dolores said. "It is not a story I am proud of. But for your sake I must tell you."

She paused, her fingers tightening on his arm, seeking reassurance.

"I was not happy here," she continued, "not with Tom. And his daughter didn't—well, we didn't get along. I wanted to go back to New Orleans, to the kind of life I knew. But I had no money of my own. And when Tom died, I found he had left little money, and half of it went to Ellen. I owned a quarter of the stage line. I asked Frank Hayes to buy me out, but he refused. I tried to get others interested."

She paused to take a long breath. "Then, a few weeks ago, Frank came to see me." She reddened slightly. "He told me he was in love with me, that he had not wanted to buy me out because he knew I would go back to New Orleans. He told me to wait. He had something big planned, something that would mean a lot of money—much more than the stage line was worth."

"When was this?"

"A week before he disappeared." Her eyes met Jeff's with innocent candor. "He told me not to worry if he went away for a short while—he said he'd get in touch with me as soon as he could—"

She got up and walked to the window and turned to face Jeff. "I know it sounds—well, disloyal to my husband. But Tom had been dead a year—and I'm still young, Jeff."

Her voice was defiant. "I've hated Jericho ever since I arrived here. I wanted Tom to sell out. And when Frank Hayes came to see me—"

She stopped, studying Jeff's bleak face. Then she

came to him, stood close. She put her hands on his shoulders. "I don't care about Frank now. I didn't know he planned to rob his own stage line. I want you to believe that."

Jeff nodded, his voice bleak. "I believe you."

Her hands slipped from his shoulder. She picked up her bag and turned to him.

"Was Frank a friend of yours?"

Jeff shook his head. His voice held little emotion. "Only a matter of business, like I told you."

She paused at the door. "I hope nothing happens to Frank's boy. I don't believe he had any part in his father's plans at all. I'm sure he didn't."

Jeff opened the door for her without comment. She turned in the hallway.

"I'll see you again, Jeff?"

He nodded. She smiled, then was gone.

Jeff closed the door and stood in the room, the poker game forgotten. There was a bleakness in his face that deepened as he reviewed the moments just past.

It had been a good act, but was it the truth? Outside, he could hear the distant cries of a baffled mob, a few mild shots expended out of frustration.

He blew out the light and raised the shade and stood by the darkened window, gazing out into the night. He had found Dolores. He should be exulting, making plans. . . . But there was no stir of excitement in him; only a bitter melancholy.

He thought of Frank Hayes. If Dolores' story were true, it settled the matter of Frank's dishonesty. It added the missing element of motive to his disappearance and would be convincing to any jury. What a man might not do for a quarter of a million dollars, he might do for a woman.

And yet what had Dolores to gain by telling him about the affair between herself and Frank Hayes? Somewhat cynically, Jeff was inclined to believe that Dolores would make few moves without that thought in mind.

Was she part of the pattern to damn Frank Hayes and his son Bill? Jeff had seen the terrible hatred in Howard Pope's face at the mention of Frank Hayes—and that hatred had extended to Frank's son. Why? The mine owner had reason to hate Frank, believing as he did that Frank had robbed him of a quarter of a million dollars. But a reasonable man would have balked at abetting the lynching of Frank's son.

Jeff's lips twisted with bleak anger. He felt like chucking the whole thing and riding out of Jericho on the double. But there was a scared boy hiding out in the hills who needed him. And, yes, there was also Dolores. The anticipation was gone, and the dream; she would never haunt him again. But she, too, needed him.

Why, he didn't know. But of this he was sure—she needed him to get out of Jericho.

EIGHT

A TALK WITH CHANDLER

THE WIND SHIFTED DURING THE NIGHT, AND THE
insistent patter of sand ebbed. By morning it had died
down, and the silence lay like a crouched animal,
waiting for the dawn.

In the semi-darkness, a lean figure on a borrowed
horse rode into Jericho. A walnut-handled Colt filled
his right holster—his left rode empty on his thigh.

Only a mongrel dog, sniffing the corner of the Gold
Nugget, saw Quincey ride by. The gunman turned the
horse towards the rail of Baldy's Bar & Pool Hall. He
left the animal nosing the tie-rack and went wobbling
down the alley to the rear of the false-fronted structure, where he kicked impatiently at a door.

Quincey was in a dangerous mood. His jaw was
swollen to twice its normal size; he looked like a
gangly boy with the mumps. Pain throbbed steadily,
clubbing the back of his head, sending waves of
nausea through him.

At the fourth savage kick he heard a voice growl
steeply, "Wait a minute—"

A bolt rasped, and the door opened cautiously.
Quincey kicked it viciously and shouldered his way
inside, ignoring the man's cry of pain. At the sound of
a muttered curse, he whirled, his hand heeling his Colt
butt.

73

The old swamper and night watchman choked on his anger. "I didn't know it was you, Quincey!"

It was an effort for Quincey to talk. Sweat beaded his upper lip. "I'm going to sleep here. I don't want anyone to know I'm back, except Mr. Pope."

The old man nodded quickly. "Sure, sure, Quincey." He opened the door to his small, scantily furnished cubbyhole behind the bar. "You want anything?"

The gunman was already peeling off his coat, unbuckling his gun belts. "A bottle of whisky," he whispered thickly. "And leave me alone."

The old man scurried around the bar and returned with a bottle. Quincey waited for him to leave, then kicked the door shut. The pain was making him half-crazy—he could barely move his lower jaw. A savage gust of hate for the man who had done this to him shook his lean frame.

He took a long pull at the bottle, and then another. He shuddered and coughed, and tears of pain filled his eyes.

As the contents lowered in the bottle, the pain began to ebb. He could feel the blood pulse in his jaw, but somehow the pain no longer registered in his head. He took another last long swallow; then the cumulative effects of the two-thirds of a fifth of 90-proof whisky reached up and slugged him. He fell back on the unmade cot and passed out, the whisky bottle slipping from his fingers, making a small thump on the floor.

He was still in that comatose position when the old

74

swamper looked in on him two hours later. He softly closed the door and went out to tell Howard Pope that Quincey was back in town.

Jeff Carter emerged from the hotel and walked up the street past the stage office. A coach had come in during the night, and fresh horses moved restlessly in their harness. Jeff wondered who was running the stage line now, and how long it would continue in operation. Somehow he couldn't see Dolores Bendore as having an active part in it.

Several passengers were waiting to board the coach. Pringle, the cigar salesman, waved at Jeff, and Jeff nodded a greeting. The fat man kept looking after Carter, a worried look in his eyes.

Jeff crossed the street and went into the barbershop next to the stone bank. He found the chair unoccupied and seated himself, relaxing while the barber, an angular, red-faced man with hairy forearms and a glistening bald head, cut his hair. He was in the midst of a shave when boots thumped over the threshold and a chair creaked under the weight of a man's body.

The barber had maintained a stony silence with Jeff, but he opened up at the newcomer's arrival.

"They find Joe's bay yet, Kenny?" He was shaving under Jeff's ear as he talked.

The newcomer shifted his long legs. "Nope. Joe borrowed a cayuse at the stable and headed back for the ranch this morning." The man hawked and looked around for the cuspidor. "Darned town is going to blazes," he growled. "The stage disappears with a

75

quarter of a million in gold. The town marshal disappears with his prisoner. Joe's horse disappears while he's getting a few drinks." Kenny shook his head. "I'm keeping a close eye on anything belonging to me from here on, George."

The barber finished with Jeff, and the tall Wells Fargo man paid him. He paused to straighten his tie before the mirror, and Kenny, rising and heading for the chair Jeff had just vacated, said, "Hey! Ain't you the feller who tangled with Quincey?"

Jeff turned a cold eye on the man. "You a friend of his?"

"Not me!" Kenny disclaimed hurriedly. "But in case you don't know it yet, Quincey's side-kick is in town. The Faraday Kid."

Jeff's smile held no warmth. "Thanks."

The barber stared after him as Kenny settled slowly in the chair. "You take a good look at him, Kenny?" he asked. "Strangest eyes I ever looked into. Reminded me of a cougar's at night." He shivered. "I was plumb careful shaving *him,* I tell you."

Jeff paused on the walk outside to roll himself a smoke. He found himself facing the stage office, and his glance moved idly from the driver getting ready to roll, to the building behind the stagecoach. The stage office stood apart from the building, separated from the main structure on the west by a narrow, boarded-up alley and a wider entrance on the east which led to sheds and stables in the rear.

It was a two-storey structure with three windows facing the street on the second floor. Evidently the second floor had provided living quarters for someone. Curtains decorated the windows.

Jeff's glance moved idly along these windows, then slid back swiftly as he caught the slight movement of curtains in the middle window. For a moment he thought he had spotted a small face pressed against the panes—then it was gone.

He took a deep drag on his cigarette, a frown making a deep crease between his eyes. He would have sworn that face belonged to Topah!

Jeff tossed his butt into the street and turned to the bank on the corner. He recalled that Calvin Chandler had been the only man in town to stand by Bill Hayes, and he had an idea the banker might be able to fill in the pattern he was trying to put together.

The bank was comparatively empty when he entered. A woman was at the teller's window, waiting while the narrow-shouldered man behind the cage bars counted out a few crisp bills. She turned and walked past him on her way out, and Jeff asked of the teller: "Is Mr. Chandler in?"

The teller made a motion towards a closed door behind the small railing. "I'll tell him you wish to see him, Mr.—"

But Jeff was already pushing the railing gate aside and walking to the door. He knocked once and went inside without waiting for Chandler's acknowledgement.

The banker was seated behind a plain mahogany desk, his face buried in his hands. He looked up as he heard Jeff come inside, his body stiffening against his

77

chair. His eyes met Jeff's with bitter questioning, and Jeff saw the livid bruise high on his right cheek.

"I don't usually see anyone in my office without a previous appointment," he stated coldly.

Jeff walked up to his desk, put his palms down on it and leaned close to Chandler.

"I'll put your mind at rest," he said cheerfully. "I'm in town for Wells Fargo."

Chandler studied him for a long moment, then settled back in his chair, a soft sigh escaping him.

"If you are, then you're just the last of a long line," he said bitterly.

Jeff took a letter from his pocket and handed it to Chandler. The banker read it without showing much emotion, then handed it back.

"John Sturvesant has a lot of faith in you," he commented quietly.

Jeff shrugged. "It's a gamble, either way," he admitted.

Chandler remembered that Jeff had been sitting in the poker game with Pope last night; he had been impressed with Jeff's playing. But, he reflected heavily, a man would need more than a fine hand at cards to get to the root of the trouble here.

"I'll do what I can to help," he told Jeff. "But I think you came too late."

"If you're thinking of Bill Hayes," Jeff said, "he's safe." He smiled at the look in Chandler's eyes as he told the banker of last night's quick shuffle.

"Bill should be out of trouble—for a few days at least."

78

"Thank God!" Chandler breathed. He waved Jeff to a chair. "Sit down. You're the best news I've heard since Frank—since he disappeared."

Carter pulled a chair closer to the desk. "Sturvesant didn't believe that Frank willingly disappeared, Mr. Chandler. In fact, he had been invited to Frank's son's wedding just a few days before. I came to find out what happened."

Chandler shook his head. "Everybody in town knows what happened—or they think they do." He made a motion with his hands. "I don't believe for one minute that Frank Hayes stole that money. But, as you may have observed, I'm in the minority in this town. Howard Pope is sure that Frank stole his gold shipment, and he's doing everything he can to smear the Hayes family. Sometimes I think he's gone crazy with the idea of revenge for what happened."

Jeff frowned. "Any reason why Pope should hate Frank Hayes, besides loss of his gold shipment?"

Chandler hesitated. "None that I know of. I'm sure Frank didn't know the man until he came to Jericho. They had little in common then, except in a business way, of course. But"—Chandler closed his eyes, thinking back—"Frank did seem to have something on his mind. I think there was something in his past that bothered him. But he never talked to me about it. More than once, that I know of, he'd ride out to Lost Springs Canyon—that's across the Sinks, north-west of town—and stare into the hills for hours. Bill told me about it, and I asked Frank about it. But Frank just shrugged it off."

Chandler tapped his fingers on the desk top, frowning. "If you know anything about this part of the Territory, you'll remember that Lost Springs Canyon was an Apache hideout not so long ago."

Jeff nodded that he recalled.

"Morado's bunch used it," Chandler continued. "The entrance to the canyon is just one big bog of quicksand. Old-timers say it's because of underground springs in the area."

A flash of understanding showed in Jeff's gaze. "You figgering that those bogs are deep enough to hide a stagecoach, Chandler?"

The banker started. His eyes gripped Jeff's. "Yes," he muttered. "Deep enough to hide the stage—and Frank Hayes' body!"

"Four men killed an Indian named Pete and his wife yesterday," Jeff recalled. "I saw three of those men standing in front of Baldy's Bar right after I came to town."

He described them.

"Whitey Smith is the thin one—I know he had an upper plate. Lon Derek and Tol Oliver are the other two." Chandler touched the bruise on his cheek. "I got this last night when I tried to stop Oliver from going inside the marshal's office after Bill Hayes. I didn't know then that Bill wasn't inside."

"They work for Pope?"

Chandler nodded. "I was just leaving the bank yesterday when they rode in. Must have been right after they left Pete's place. Monty was riding with them—I thought at the time he had been hurt. He was sort of slumped forward in his saddle."

"Bill said his father was friendly with the Crow family. You know why?"

"Pete used to be an Army scout, years ago," Chandler recalled. "Later he and Frank prospected this area. Frank didn't talk much about that period. But he used to send things out to Pete's shack every so often. And whenever Pete's boy, Topah, came to town, he'd hang around the stage office and the stables. Bill liked the kid."

Jeff's voice was suddenly interested. "Who lives above the stage office?"

"Nobody—now," Chandler replied. "Frank and Bill Hayes lived there. Frank liked to be near the office. He had worked hard to build up this stage line—he was proud of it."

Jeff stood up. "Thanks for the fill-in, Mr. Chandler."

He picked up his hat, and the banker said, "One more thing, Jeff. What I'm going to say has bothered me for a long time. But I didn't dare tell it to anyone before." He flushed, half-ashamed of himself. "It's not anything definite, anyway. But seeing as how you're working for Wells Fargo, and it concerns them directly—"

He paused. Jeff said: "Mrs. Bendore?"

Chandler looked surprised. "No, I wasn't thinking about her."

"How did Frank feel about her—as a partner?"

Chandler pursed his lips. "Frank didn't feel one way or another, far as I know. He thought Tom made a mistake, marrying a woman like that and bringing

81

her to a place like Jericho. But I think he figured it was Tom's business, not his." He shrugged. "Even after Tom died, she didn't bother much with the business—"

"Was Frank friendly with her?"

Chandler eyed Jeff. "If you mean what I think you mean, I'd say no. She was from another sort of world—I think Frank was a little afraid of her." He frowned. "She wanted Frank to buy her out, I know that. Frank would have, gladly—but things were going a little badly, and he wanted what money he had to give his son Bill and Ellen Bendore a good wedding."

Jeff nodded. He turned to go, and for a moment Chandler watched him, having seen something in his face that disconcerted the banker.

"Did you know Mrs. Bendore?" he asked.

Jeff turned. "A long time ago, when she was Dolores Camarillo," he said quietly.

Chandler waited a moment, but Jeff had nothing more to say on the subject. Then he remembered what he had started to tell Jeff.

"I was going to tell you about the High Life Mine when we got off on another track." He got up and walked to a large wall map of the immediate area.

He pointed with a forefinger. "Fancy name for a worthless mine, Jeff. Never paid off much, even in the beginning. And it was pretty well played out when Howard Pope and Frank Connors came to town. Connors claims to be a mining engineer. He may be. On his recommendation, Howard Pope bought the mine—

paid practically nothing for the lease and the stamp mill. Everyone in town thought Pope was a fool. But two weeks later he came to town with the news that his men had struck a new vein—almost pure gold!"

Chandler paused. "From the first, the High Life outfit has been a suspicious bunch. Pope keeps guards at the mine and in the stamp mill. And it wasn't long after that he began shipping gold bullion. It started a run of activity at the other abandoned mines around here, but no one else has had the same luck. However, Pope's men spend their money in town, and it helped business here, so no one asked too many embarrassing questions."

The banker made a gesture towards the wall map. "I don't say that Howard Pope didn't hit it rich in the old High Life shaft. Things like that have happened before."

Jeff nodded. "Does he still keep a guard at the mine?"

"Two men," Chandler answered. "They've got direct orders from Pope to shoot first and check later."

Jeff chuckled coldly. "I'm interested, Mr. Chandler. In fact, I think I'll try to take a look inside the High Life sometime soon."

"No one gets inside without Mr. Pope's clearance," Chandler warned.

Jeff shrugged. "Then I'll talk to him first."

Chandler held out his hand. "If I can be of more help—?"

"I'll be back," Jeff promised.

He liked the banker's firm handshake as they parted.

NINE

AN OLD SCORE TO SETTLE

THE ORIENTAL RESTAURANT ON GOLD STREET HAD yellow curtains which softened the light through its windows, diluting it as it seemed to dilute the mutter of voices within.

Jeff paused inside the doorway, letting his eyes accustom themselves to the change from the bright sunlight outside. He wanted a place where he could linger over a late breakfast while he sorted out what Chandler had told him, and decided what he was going to do with Dolores.

A short, yellow-skinned man came to him, bowing and smiling, his voice a singsong of politeness. Jeff followed the man into the room and was about to sit down when he saw Dolores Bendore.

She was seated at a rear corner table with Frank Connors. In that moment of encounter, Jeff had the distinct and unpleasant feeling that he had surprised them. Then Dolores smiled a quick welcome and waved to him, inviting Jeff to their table.

Frank Connors didn't seem pleased to see Jeff. "I didn't know you were another Wells Fargo agent," he said coldly. "And I don't think Howard's going to like it. If Sturvesant was sending another man down here, he should have been notified."

Jeff's gaze went to Dolores. She looked flustered.

"I hope I didn't give anything away, Jeff. I didn't know—"

Jeff shrugged. "No reason Mr. Connors and Mr. Pope shouldn't know, Mrs. Bendore. Anyway, I'm about convinced there's little I can do here. Frank's trail is cold—too cold for me to waste my time trying to trace him. However," he added drily, "I do expect you'll get in touch with me when you receive word from him."

"Of course, Jeff," Dolores answered readily. "I told Mr. Connors about Frank. If I had suspected what Frank Hayes had in mind at the time—well, I'm sure I wouldn't have encouraged him."

Connors' cold gaze rested on Jeff. "Odd how Bill Hayes disappeared last night, wasn't it? Shortly after you left our poker table at the Comanche, too."

"Isn't it?" Jeff agreed. "I heard the marshal vamoosed, too. Seems to me he got wind the mob was coming for his prisoner and decided to light out with Bill Hayes until things blew over." His eyes reflected a thin humor. "Smart thinking on the marshal's part, don't you think, Connors?"

The mine superintendent's mouth pinched. "Smartest thinking Bart ever did—if that's what he did last night," he agreed coldly.

He took an expensive cigar from his pocket and clipped the end with a gold cigar clipper.

"By the way, we waited two hours for you to come back last night," he added casually.

Jeff shrugged. "Thought it over and decided I couldn't afford to lose more than I had." He looked at

Dolores. "Besides, I had company. . . ."

Dolores shot a look at Connors, then put a hand on Jeff's arm. "Let's all be friends," she said quickly. "Let's forget for the moment what's happened. I want to hear about New Orleans." She turned to Jeff. "Frank's recently come from there, Jeff."

The conversation turned to more idle subjects while the waiter brought Jeff's breakfast. When it was time for coffee, Jeff automatically reached up to his pocket for the makings. His fingers encountered the cigar Pringle had given him, and he took it out and examined it. The band seemed somewhat bulky, and he slipped it free, frowning slightly as a fat-rolled strip of white paper fell beside his cup.

He unfolded it, his eyes narrowing on the tight, fine writing that appeared under his fingers.

Carter: Meet me at the Apache Wells stage stopover tomorrow. Urgent. Perry Keight. Pinkerton Agency.

The Wells Fargo man became aware of the intent look on Frank Connors' face, of Dolores' wide-eyed regard, and he slowly crumpled the note and the cigar band between his fingers.

"Beats me how some drummers will think up new angles to sell their products," he said idly. "You get one, too, Connors?"

"Get what?" Connors' voice held an odd inflection.

"Cigar. Drummer named Pringle handed me one last night at the Comanche Bar. Wrote his name and address on a slip of paper and stuck it under the band."

Connors shook his head. "Guess I don't rate a free smoke," he said dryly.

He rose and nodded to Dolores. "I must leave. I'm really sorry about your trouble with the stage line, Mrs. Bendore. I'll see what Mr. Pope can do for you after he gets that insurance check. After all, I see no reason you should be penalized for what your partner did."

He turned to Jeff, his eyes remote and unfriendly. "It might ease Quincey's humiliation slightly to know it was one of John Sturvesant's sharpshooters who manhandled him." The sneer in his voice was barely concealed. "I'll try to keep him out of your way, Mr. Carter."

"Do that." Jeff answered, and his voice was as dry as the rustling of Spanish dagger in the desert wind.

Dolores' contrite voice, after Connors left, turned Jeff's attention to her.

"I'm sorry if I gave you away, Jeff."

He studied her coldly now, remembering the first impression of intimacy between her and Connors. The mine superintendent had put on a convincing act of being surprised to learn Jeff's identity. But Jeff had a sudden hunch that since Dolores had come to him last night, Frank Connors had known, too. Connors and Howard Pope must have known all along who he was and why he was there, as he sat across the poker table from them last night at the Comanche Bar.

Was Connors behind her coming to his room? Was Dolores' story only another part of the pattern to damn Frank Hayes?

He asked her bluntly, "Just why did you tell me about Frank Hayes last night?"

Her eyes widened in a gesture he knew came automatically to her—a pose that had become a habit.

"Why, I really don't know. I imagine it's because I just naturally assumed you must have been sent here to look for Frank. So many other men have come."

Her explanation didn't satisfy Jeff, but he let it stand.

"What about Bill Hayes?"

She shook her head emphatically. "Whatever Connors and Pope might think, Jeff, I know he had nothing to do with the stage's disappearance. But it's all been such a shock to Ellen." Her voice sounded genuinely sympathetic.

"I'll bet," Jeff said curtly.

He stood up, and Dolores said quickly, "You're not leaving so soon?" Her full lips pouted. "I'm sure you're mad at me for telling Mr. Connors—"

"Not at all," Jeff assured her. "But I have just remembered I have an appointment."

"Jeff!" Her voice changed. Her lips lost their teasing pout. "Look out!" She seemed to be suddenly frightened, suddenly concerned. "I think they—" She caught herself, and ended lamely, "Just take care of yourself, Jeff."

He nodded. What she had started to tell him, and then changed her mind, he never found out.

The Faraday Kid, alias Ward Calhoun, ex-member of the old Petersen gang and out on parole, sat on a corner of Howard's Pope's desk in the High Life office. He was a lean, blond man, nail-hard and restless, with eyes that glittered impatiently under bleached brows. The Kid, orphaned at two, had spent the rest of his life getting even with the world for it.

Howard Pope sat behind his desk, his scarred face uglier than usual. Monty Breen, his shoulder bandaged, his left arm in a sling, puffed on a bad cigar. Lon Derek, physically almost the twin of the Faraday Kid, picked at his teeth with a sharpened end of a kitchen match.

They eyed Connors without comment as the superintendent came into the office. He tossed his hat on a hook and turned to Pope, his voice conveying his urgency and uneasiness.

"He's in the Oriental right now. I think he just got a message from that fat Pinkerton man, Keight." Connors wet his lips. "If Carter gets together with Keight—"

Pope interrupted him harshly: "Whitey and Tol Oliver are following the stage right now. If Keight gets off, they'll take care of him!"

He reached out and flicked tobacco ash from his desk with an irritable gesture. The Faraday Kid took the hint and slid off the desk, hitching at his gun belt.

"You say he keeps his cayuse at the Long Bar Stables?" At Connors' nod, he smiled.

Pope said coldly, "You sure you know him?"

"If he's the same gambler I ran into on a Mississippi river boat, I know him. Called himself Jeff Sharp in those days. I was just a kid working with Petersen."

"Then he'll know who you are," Connors cut in sharply. He turned to Pope. "I don't like it, Howard. If he starts making a connection between the old Petersen gang and us—"

"Don't worry about the connection!" the Faraday Kid snapped. "Monty and I will take care of Jeff. He'll never even leave town!"

Connors shook his head. "That's what we've got to avoid." He looked at Pope. "One more killing in town, and the next thing we'll have a company of Rangers on our necks!"

The Faraday Kid didn't like Connors; his edgy voice said so. "I said I'd handle it, Mr. Connors! Jeff won't be shot; he'll be trampled to death!" He sneered at Connors' puzzled frown. "Accident, of course."

He turned and prodded Monty towards the back door. "Come on, lard butt!" he growled. "Let's get a move on."

Connors sank slowly into a chair as Monty and the Kid left the office. Derek eyed the superintendent curiously, still working at his teeth.

Pope chuckled. "Relax, Frank. The Kid's planned this move since he heard that another Wells Fargo man was in town. We won't have to worry about Carter after today. And as soon as that Wells Fargo insurance check comes, we'll blow."

He turned to stare through the window, and his voice harshened. "They'll never know what happened to Frank Hayes!"

The late morning sun lay warm in the alley leading

90

to the Long Bar Stables. Jeff came towards the big barn at a swinging walk and looked in at Jake's living quarters. Jake was nowhere in sight.

He paused briefly, and in that moment he heard a man's heavy voice lifted in angry cursing, the sharp crack of a whip, and the maddened hurt whistling of a horse as he lunged and kicked within his stall.

Jeff turned to the big open stable door, wondering if Jake was mistreating one of the animals. Sunlight made an odd wedge through the doorway, but the rest of the big, sour-smelling barn was almost dark in contrast. The Wells Fargo man stopped just inside, instinctively moving to get his back against the walls. Slowly his eyes accustomed themselves to the gloom.

A line of wooden-sided stalls took up three-quarters of the big barn. A newly-painted gig and harness took up the rest of the space, with alfalfa bales and feed bags stacked in an open-fronted loft above the stalls.

There was one man in sight, but he wasn't Jake. He was a burly, heavy-hipped man with his left arm in a sling, whom Jeff immediately recognized. He was wielding a whip with his right hand, lashing at a rangy red roan whose wild kicking had already splintered the two wide boards at his rear.

Jeff's eyes narrowed, and he alertly surveyed what he could see of the barn's interior. This man was one of the four riders who had killed Pete, Frank Hayes' Indian guide; the man Calvin Chandler had identified as Monty Breen.

At the far end of the stall line, Jeff's palomino recognized him and tugged impatiently at his halter rope. Then he stood still, his ears pricked sharply and his head turned to look into the shadows of the empty stall next to him.

It was a bird-dog signal, and a cold smile formed on Jeff's lips. He eased away from the wall, moving towards the burly man wielding the whip. His approach was silent, and Monty did not hear him until Jeff's flat voice jerked him around.

"That's no way to treat a horse, even if it does belong to you!"

Monty looked Jeff up and down with an insolent sneer. "Go soak yore head, feller!" He turned back to the roan and put his weight behind the cut of his whip.

Jeff's hand fell on Monty's bandaged shoulder, whirling his around. Monty's sudden curse was sharp with pain. He tried to pull his whip arm back, and Jeff wrenched the whip out of his grasp.

"I reckon a taste of this ought to—"

"Drop it, Jeff!"

The voice came from down the stall line, from the shadows around the palomino's pen. A cold, impatient voice mirrored the restlessness of the man himself.

Jeff dropped the whip and turned slightly to face the lean figure of the Faraday Kid. Jeff did not know him as the Kid. He remembered this man as Ward Calhoun, one-time member of the notorious Petersen gang, and surprise ran through him, while a part of his mind began to fit this gunslinger into the complex pattern of Frank Hayes' disappearance.

Monty picked up the whip Jeff had dropped.

Behind the Wells Fargo man the hurt roan quivered nervously, ready to let fly with deadly hoofs at anything within reach.

Monty's glance flicked to the trembling animal as he raised the whip again, and in that instant Jeff understood the grim intentions of the burly-shouldered man, and realized, too, why Ward Calhoun didn't shoot.

The blond gunman had his back to Jeff's palomino's stall, a gun in his fist, and his voice bit through the stable quiet, hard and restless. "I've got an old score to settle with him, Monty! Give him a taste of that whip for me!"

Monty grinned. His arm cut down viciously, and in that moment Jeff gave a sharp whistle and lunged forward.

He had raised that palomino from a colt and trained it himself. The horse lunged against the boards at Jeff's whistle, fighting to pull free of the halter rope, to get to the man who called him. The impact of his body against the boards jarred Calhoun off balance. He stumbled, and a reflex tightened his trigger finger, sending a bullet up into the rafters.

Monty's whip whistled through the air and wrapped itself around Jeff's upthrust left arm. The Wells Fargo man yanked back with savage strength, and Monty, gripping hard on the handle, was jerked forward.

Jeff side-stepped the stumbling man and cuffed him with a backhand swipe, sending Monty plunging towards the splintered boards of the roan's stall. Jeff's movements were continuous. He was whirling, lifting his holstered Colt, thumbing the hammer, all in one fluid motion. The racking explosions hammered the silence in the gloomy stables.

Calhoun, alias the Faraday Kid, came up on his toes, a shocked look in his pale eyes. Whatever he was looking for, he was through searching now.

Behind Jeff, the maltreated roan was lunging and kicking, its whistling shrill above the fading explosions. A body hit Carter just above the bend of his knees, knocking him off balance. He twisted like a cat, balanced momentarily on his hands and knees, his Colt still in his hand.

Monty was a shapeless mass under him. The fingers of Jeff's left hand felt suddenly sticky and wet, and he took one look at Monty's face and turned away.

The roan's flying hoofs must have caught Monty squarely in his face!

Jeff straightened and headed for the palomino in the far stall. He had a sudden feeling that time was slipping past, that he was going to be too late to meet Perry Keight, Pinkerton detective. And Keight, he thought bleakly, would have been able to fill in the last threads in the strange pattern Jeff was piecing together here!

TEN

DEATH STOP AT APACHE WELLS

CALEB PETERS WATCHED THE STAGE FROM JERICHO TOP the rise and head for the station of Apache Wells. He turned without hurry and poked his head inside the long adobe structure. "It's coming," he yelled to Maria, his Mexican wife, who was busy in the small kitchen at the far end of the way station.

Then he turned and walked out into the sun-beaten yard to meet the stage as it swung in off the road.

Caleb had been with Tom Bendore and Frank Hayes since they had started the Sinks run—an old driver whose rheumatism had taken him from the jolting seat to this less arduous post.

He didn't believe Frank Hayes had run off with the Wells Fargo box, but he had no explanation for Frank's disappearance. He wasn't happy about the future. The stage was making its last runs, and he knew he'd be out of a job unless someone else took over the line.

Hank Toolin, the driver, pulled the coach up under the shade of the lone oak by the corral and stepped down from the seat, bringing out a lint-covered piece of chewing tobacco and taking a healthy bite from it. Caleb joined him, and together they watched the passengers step out of the coach: three men and two women, both too heavy and too old to keep his interest.

"Chow inside the station," he said mechanically, and watched them file wearily towards the building.

Perry Keight lingered behind the others and glanced back along the road to Jericho. He saw no sign of Jeff Carter, and a sinking feeling brought sweat to his already moist face. He should have been more direct, instead of trying to be clever with a message in a cigar band, he thought dismally. But he had known he was being watched, and a direct approach might have given the Wells Fargo man away. John Sturvesant had written him that Jeff was coming, and after that meeting on the hotel staircase he had glanced at the hotel register and noticed that Jeff had signed himself Jim Sharp.

Perry was a methodical man with a mind for detail and a retentive memory. He had seen Jeff Carter once, during the Petersen gang trial in Denver, and Jeff's features (although Jeff had never been part of that band) had been imprinted in his mind.

Now he waited several long moments, but the trail remained empty. He walked inside the cool adobe station and found a place at the long plank table. Caleb's daughter, a pigtailed girl of about twelve, served.

The stop-over lasted only long enough to change horses. But all except the women were through with the noon meal when the driver stuck his head inside the door and yelled: "Let's get rollin'!"

The others got up and moved to the door. The Pinkerton man followed, but he did not enter the coach.

"I'm staying over," he decided. "I forgot something

in Jericho. I'll catch the next stage back."

The driver shrugged. He reached up on the luggage rack and tossed Keight's pigskin bag down at his feet.

The Pinkerton man waited until the stage rolled out of sight; then he picked up his bag and started back to the station. Caleb was in the corral, tending to the tired team animals.

Perry paused in the doorway to glance at the trail to Jericho and saw two riders coming at an easy lope. A swift fear twisted Keight's mouth out of shape.

I should have expected this, he thought bitterly.

For a moment he was tempted to make a run for it, and almost at once he knew it would be a futile try. He gauged the distance of the two men and then turned quickly and went inside the station.

Caleb's daughter had cleared the table and was inside the kitchen helping her mother. Keight's eyes moved swiftly over the room and settled on a wooden box, its lid secured by a padlock, fastened to the wall beside an old roll-top desk. The word "Mail" was painted on the face of the box.

The Pinkerton man dropped his bag on the table and opened it. A Smith & Wesson .38 pistol lay on top of a shirt. He picked it up, checked it and thrust it against his paunch, under his belt. He rummaged deeper and brought out an unsealed envelope which he now sealed and to which he added a stamp. He had written this note on the stage, and he wondered if Jeff would be able to read the scrawl. He started to write Jeff's name on the envelope, then remembered in time to make it "Jim Sharp, care of the Tower Hotel, Jericho".

He dropped the letter into the mailbox and, turning, caught the girl peering at him from the kitchen doorway. He shrugged and walked back to the table, and was just settling himself in the corner when he heard the riders pull up outside.

They came in together, drawing guns. Tol Oliver stopped at the far end of the long table. Whitey drifted off to one side. The girl had disappeared inside the kitchen.

Oliver said flatly, "You should have stayed on that stage, Hawkshaw! It would have been healthier!"

Keight took a deep breath. "I don't know what you're talking about, fellers." The sweat glistened on his face. "I'm a drummer from St Louis."

Whitey's gun bucked in his hand. He fired again, almost casually, and Oliver growled, "You could have waited until I had my say, blast you!"

They turned away and climbed into the saddle. Caleb was running towards the station, gun in hand, from the corral. He stopped as they wheeled around; they eyed him briefly, then rode away.

After they had gone, Caleb went inside.

Jeff Carter arrived a half-hour later. Caleb Peters had pulled Keight's body from behind the table. The Pinkerton man lay on the floor with a blanket covering him.

Caleb didn't want to talk at first. But John Sturvesant's letter of authority, backed by the grimness of Jeff's face, loosened his tongue.

"Recognized both of them," Caleb admitted. "Whitey Smith and Tol Oliver." He made a gesture to the doorway. "I didn't see what happened, though. I was outside, in the corral, when I heard the shots. I hadn't even seen them ride up."

Jeff stood beside the body. Whatever Keight had wanted to tell him, he'd never know now. But he knew who had killed him. And he knew where to find them!

Caleb's wife and daughter watched from the kitchen doorway. The girl spoke then, swiftly, in Mexican.

Caleb turned to Jeff. "Juanita says she saw the fat man drop something in the mailbox just before the two men came in."

Jeff spun around. "Let's take a look at it!"

The station man hesitated, then hauled out a key ring and unlocked the mailbox. There was one letter inside. He read the name on it: "Jim Sharp, care of the Tower Hotel—"

"That's me," Jeff said, took the letter from Caleb and ripped the flap open.

The penciled words were badly scrawled; he had to read them slowly to make sense of the message:

Jeff—In case I miss you, I'm writing this down. I think they suspect who I am. I saw the Faraday Kid this morning. He's Ward Calhoun, one of the old Petersen gang. He'll remember you. There are a few more of the Petersen gang in town. They work for Howard Pope. Does that mean

anything? The Petersen gang, as you know, spe-
cialized in train hold-ups. Most of what they
stole was in gold bullion. The High Life mine
was played out. When Howard Pope took it over,
it began to pay off. How come? Who saw the
vein he claims to have found in the old shaft?
Ask Bill Hayes if his father ever prospected the
Captains? Who with? Does he know the old
Apache Way into Lost Springs Canyon?

It was signed: *Perry.*

Jeff slipped the envelope and its contents into his pocket. There was little in Perry Keight's note which he had not already known, but the Pinkerton man's terse comments served to bring the pattern into focus. Ward Calhoun had been a member of the Petersen gang. Keight said there were more of the old bunch in Jericho.

Jeff smiled grimly. Petersen was dead. But someone could have gathered together what was left of the old bunch. A man like Howard Pope, or Frank Connors.

The pattern was now bringing out the sharp design. Stolen bullion was hard to explain. But stolen bullion that disappeared into a closely guarded mine and came worth eventually as the product of that mine was something else again.

But where did Frank Hayes fit in? And Dolores Bendore?

He stood for a moment, facing the uncertain future, not wanting to know. Not about Dolores.

Then he turned to Caleb. "When's the next stage through here for Jericho?"

Jeff indicated the blanket-covered body. "Get him on it, tagged for the undertaker. I'll notify his office myself."

He left Caleb staring down at the body, frowning. The palomino snorted as Jeff mounted and swung him around towards the low hills that separated the station from the town of Jericho.

ELEVEN

THE BETRAYAL

Dolores Bendore knocked gently on the bedroom door and then, when it went unanswered, opened it and went inside.

Ellen lay across her bed, fully clothed, her face resting on her forearms. She must have heard Dolores come inside, but she didn't move. She felt frightened and alone, and the older woman provided no comfort. She and Dolores lived as strangers in her father's house.

Dolores eyed the girl with some sympathy. "Dinner's ready," she said quietly.

Ellen's voice was muffled. "I'm not hungry."

Dolores crossed to the bed and sat down beside her. She put a hand gently on Ellen's shoulder. "You didn't have breakfast," she reminded her. Then, as Ellen remained silent, she added, "Starving yourself won't bring Bill back."

Ellen rolled away from her and sat up; her eyes were red from recent weeping.

"You'd like that, wouldn't you?" she cried.

Dolores' small smile tightened on her lips. But she was genuinely sorry for the girl.

"I'd like to see you happy," she said.

"Then find Bill," Ellen said bitterly. She brushed a hand through her hair, knowing how she must look and resenting this cool, beautifully dressed, beautifully groomed woman who had married her father but never really tried to understand his daughter.

"Scolding me won't help," Dolores said. "Nor will your crying. If I knew what happened to young Bill—"

"Mr. Connors knows. You can ask him!"

Dolores stiffened, visibly nettled. She had not wanted a scene with the girl; her gesture in coming here had not been one of deep concern. Since Tom Bendore had died, she had been looking for a way out of Jericho, and now she had found it. She shrugged, her smile slipping from her face. She pulled her hand back and started to get up.

"I know what's been going on between you and Mr. Connors," the girl said. "Ever since he came here you've been playing up to him—"

"I wasn't aware it was supposed to be a secret," Dolores said acidly. Then, "Your father's been dead a year, Ellen. And I don't like being a widow."

She walked to the door, then looked back. The girl appeared so miserable it touched her, and she said more gently, "Maybe you'll feel better later. I'll come back."

She closed the door, and Ellen turned without answering and lay across the bed, emotion bringing muffled sobs.

Dolores crossed to the kitchen and looked in where a Mexican housekeeper and cook was setting two places at the table. She caught the woman's eye, shook her head and turned away, walking slowly into the front room.

103

She heard the rider pull up in front of the house and, curious, parted the lace curtains to see who it was. It was too early for Frank Connors.

The tall man striding towards the door brought back a rush of memories. She let the curtain drop back into place and stood there undecided, torn between the past and the present.

The knocker on the front door sent its call through the house. Dolores turned and motioned away the Mexican housekeeper who was coming to answer it.

"I'll get it," she said, and stopped briefly by a gold-framed mirror to look at herself before opening the door.

Jeff looked tired and dusty and not gay as he stood on the stoop. Perry Keight's death still nagged at him. But he managed a smile as he took off his hat.

"May I come in?"

Dolores stepped back and closed the door behind him. They went into the front room. Jeff's appraisal was cursory.

"Is Ellen in?"

Dolores' eyes arched in a surprise she could not conceal. "Ellen?"

"Miss Bendore," Jeff said impatiently. "Is she in?"

Dolores nodded. "But she isn't feeling well."

Jeff said, "Maybe what I have to tell her will help her." He smiled tiredly. "It's about Bill."

"Oh!" Dolores said, turning. "I'll get her."

Jeff looked around the room as Dolores left. It was furnished simply and, like most front rooms he had visited, didn't look lived in. There was nothing of

Dolores in the room, no imprint of her personality. Only the faint and fading scent of lilacs indicated her presence there.

He stood by the window, looking out through the veiling curtains, and felt the tiredness ease in him. He had been slick and smooth, and, as John Sturvesant had reminded him, a lot of laughs once. So had Dolores. He had spent his winnings on her, as had other men, but he had always felt that with him, for Dolores, it had been not only the money, the good times at the *Chat Duclaine,* the horse races. Now he wasn't so sure.

Lost in reverie, he didn't see Dolores and Ellen come up behind him. Ellen's voice was tired and held an undercurrent of weeping. "Did you want to see me?"

Jeff turned and gravely eyed the girl, whose reddened eyes confirmed what her voice conveyed. He nodded.

"I'm sorry I didn't get a chance to see you before this. I know you're worried about Bill. I know where he is. He's safe."

Ellen's eyes remained on him, searching his face. Hope came slowly, struggling through a long night of despair.

"You—you're sure?"

"Take my word for it. I'll bring him back tomorrow, now that the lynch fever seems to have died down."

Ellen gave a small grateful cry of thankfulness, then ran to him, threw her arms around his neck, and hugged him. Standing back, Dolores smiled faintly at Jeff's momentary discomfiture.

Jeff said: "If you feel up to it, Ellen, I'd like to ask you a few questions."

Ellen glanced at Dolores, then nodded. To Dolores she said, "I'm sorry about the way I acted."

Dolores smiled. "I'll tell Rosa you're ready to eat something now."

Ellen said, "After I talk to Mr. Carter."

Dolores went into the kitchen, and Ellen continued, "I don't know how I can help you—"

"Did your father ever speak about Frank Hayes? About Frank's past?"

She shook her head. "They got along well together. Bill and his father often had supper with us. They talked mostly of plans for expanding the stage line now that the threat of the spur railroad was gone."

"Did your father ever have any trouble with Frank Hayes?" Jeff's voice was level. "Did he ever talk of selling out?"

"No. The line was making money. Not enough to make either Dad or Frank Hayes wealthy, but we were comfortable." She paused. "The only time they had any"—she hesitated, then went on—"any difficulty was when Father brought home his new wife."

She didn't see Dolores come up behind her, but reacted to the older woman's incisive tone: "I told Jeff about that, Ellen."

Ellen colored. "I didn't mean to imply anything, Dolores."

Jeff cut in, "I'm sure Dolores knows that." He

looked at Dolores, his eyes warning her.

Dolores shrugged. "I was here when Frank and his son came over. I never heard Frank mention anything about his past, either."

Ellen looked from Dolores to Jeff, and tears started in her eyes again. "I don't care what Bill's father did. I just want to go away with Bill—forget all that's happened."

She turned and ran from the room, and they heard her bedroom door close. Dolores was silent for a long moment; then: "I guess it has been a nightmare for her, Jeff."

"What about you?" Jeff's voice was even.

Dolores shrugged. "Not much better. But then, I never expected much. . . ."

She walked with Jeff to the door. "Oh, at first I was intrigued. Jericho"—she smiled faintly—"it even had a faintly wicked connotation. And I had never been west of Houston." She sighed. "Jeff, I never realized that sand and alkali and hot bare hills could be so ugly. And the people—oh, they're civil enough. But the men look at me as though I were some strange animal. And the women—" Her lips curled with faint distaste. "I should never have come here."

Jeff took her into his arms. "I have a job to finish here. If it works out the way I think it will, I should be done with it tomorrow night. Then I'll be taking you home with me."

"Home?" Her eyes held a velvet shadow.

"A horse ranch up north. Home isn't big, but it's comfortable. And it can be enlarged. I raise horses."

He smiled. "You loved horses."

"Only at the races," she murmured dreamily. "A pink parasol shading me from the sun; the excitement of the race-track; the money wagered; the fun at the *Chat Duclaine* afterward."

She looked up at him, the present coming back, stiffening her. "How can you feel content on a horse ranch?" she asked bitterly. "You were the most fascinating gambler I knew."

"I'm still gambling," he said quietly. "On you." He lifted her face up to him, his hands gentle. "You will come with me?"

She didn't answer, and after a moment Jeff kissed her. Her eyes closed, and a soft sigh escaped her.

"I have a couple of messages to send out, if the telegraph office is still open," he said. "Then I've got some business at the High Life mine. But I'll be back tomorrow."

Dolores watched Jeff leave, mounting and riding off into the teeth of the slowly rising wind. She hated that wind and the ubiquitous sand and the irritating monotony of it all. But for the moment she was strangely stirred and at peace; almost, she thought wryly, with a sort of schoolgirl's contentment.

She was about to turn back into the house when she saw Frank Connors come up the walk. He stopped and looked off in the direction Jeff had ridden; then he came on, a well-dressed, handsome man but with no softness in him.

As he came up the walk to the front steps, she saw

that his face was dark and jealous, and she knew instantly that he had seen Jeff leave.

Entering, he strode up to her and gripped her arms, his fingers rough and hurting.

"What was he doing here?"

Displeasure flared in Dolores' eyes. Whatever she was, she had never been cheap. Men handled her gently and with politeness.

"Frank!" she said harshly. "Don't ever do that again!"

His eyes locked on hers, and after a moment he released her arm and his glance shifted. He took a deep breath, his anger fading.

"I'm sorry, Dolores. I guess I'm jealous of every man who looks at you."

"I told you about Jeff," she said. "I knew him a long time ago, in New Orleans."

"What was he doing here?"

Her lips framed a small sad smile. "I think he just asked me to marry him."

Frank's face congested. "Marry him?"

Dolores' voice lowered as she remembered Ellen was in the house. "Yes."

Frank held himself under control with an effort. But his voice was strained. "What did you tell him?"

She closed her eyes. Jeff's lean face appeared before her, and she said softly, "It's the best offer I've had since I came here, Frank."

"I'm offering the same thing," Frank replied. His voice was cold. "Only I'm throwing in my cut of a quarter of a million dollars. And New Orleans."

Her eyes widened, and she studied him. "Frank," she whispered, "you're sure?"

He nodded. "Soon as that Wells Fargo insurance check comes in, I'm through with Pope!"

Dolores shuddered. "I'm glad, Frank. I never liked the way he looked at me."

Frank's lips tightened. "Nor I. Not any of them." He took her into his arms. "We don't belong here, you and I. All Howard Pope ever meant was a chance at money, real money."

He kissed her, then released her. "Wait a few more days. It won't be long now."

"That's what Jeff said," she murmured.

"Jeff?" His voice was angry.

"He said his job would be done here by tomorrow. He was going to send some wires to somebody; then he was riding out to the mine."

"The High Life?" Frank bit off the question.

She nodded; startled at his tone, she said, "What did he mean?"

But Frank was turning away, his stride just short of a running pace.

TWELVE

MESSAGE INTERCEPTED

JEFF CARTER FRESHENED UP AT THE HOTEL, THEN RODE on to the telegraph office, a sagging one-room clapboard shack on a siding about a quarter of a mile from town. A spur track, drifted over, ran alongside it, terminating at the foundations of what once had been a warehouse. The structural wood had long since been carted off by Jericho's inhabitants for use as firewood. This had occurred years ago, and for a time the telegraph office, too, had been abandoned and seemed likely to suffer the fate of the warehouse. Lately there had been talk, since Pope's reopening of the High Life mine, of the T & P Railroad rebuilding and maintaining the spur line, but it had been just talk.

Jeff dismounted by the closed door. It was padlocked, and the small rim of sand against the bottom seemed to indicate that it had not been opened recently. He glanced up at the wire coming down from the tilted fifteen-foot pole, terminating at an insulator and passing inside. The wind sang a mournful dirge along the copper strand.

The telegraph office was closed, he was convinced, and Jeff was about to give up when he noticed a figure coming towards him from a shack he had not immediately noticed set some distance back in a *barranca*. Behind the man he could see a mule dozing in the scant shade afforded by a *ramada*.

The man wore a stovepipe hat and a frayed Prince Albert coat, and he kept a hand clamped on the lid of his hat to keep it from blowing away.

His name was Zebediah Smith, but he was known locally as 'Wireless' Smith, and few people remembered his real name.

As he came up to the telegraph shack, Jeff noticed with some surprise that the man was not as old as he had at first appeared. Fortyish, perhaps, but his gray-shot stubble of beard was as deceiving as the mildness in his blue eyes.

Smith said cheerfully enough, "Saw you ride up. You expecting a wire?"

"Sending," Jeff answered. His tone sounded dubious, and Smith felt impelled to explain.

"Don't get much business these days," he said, unlocking the padlock. He looked owlishly wise. "But the super of the T & P told me they've got big plans for Jericho, as soon as the High Life mine reopens." He stepped inside, and Jeff followed. "Yessir," he continued, walking to his desk, "big plans. Place'll be jumpin' six months from now."

He didn't believe it himself, and his voice said so. Jeff looked around the shack. There was fine sand on the floor, sifted through the siding. The fine layer was everywhere. Smith sat down and blew sand from the sender key, and Jeff said, "Is the line to the county seat open?"

"It is," Smith replied, "if this cussed wind hasn't blown down a couple of poles down the line. Not too bad right here, but farther down the Sinks, by Yellow-jacket Pass, it blows a real humdinger."

He looked at Jeff. "Stranger in Jericho, eh?"

"Passing through," Jeff said idly, and added: "You going to check the line?"

Smith fisted the key and tapped out a routine check signal, and a few minutes later received the all clear.

He indicated a small counter against the wall. "Must be a pencil and some message blanks in them pigeonholes. I'm ready as soon as you are."

Jeff scribbled out a message to John Sturvesant in Denver, asking that he get in touch with the regional U.S. marshal's office. He had evidence he wanted to turn over to a man from the marshal's office, and he suggested that John get a federal officer down to Jericho immediately. He also mentioned Perry Keight's death and suggested that Sturvesant get in touch with Keight's agency.

He signed it and handed it to the telegrapher. "Send it collect."

Smith took the message, glanced at it, then back at Jeff. "You want to wait for an answer?"

"I'll be back for it," Jeff told him.

He waited a moment as Smith placed the message in front of him and began to send it on relay through Downey. Smith seemed oddly fidgety. He shuffled a bit under the desk with his legs, stopped, then tried again.

Jeff was on his way out when the line went dead. He turned.

"Just a loose connection," Smith said apologeti-

113

cally. "I'll get it fixed in no time."

Jeff nodded and went outside. The wind was picking up. It would be a long uncomfortable ride to the High Life. He could see the hills where the mine was located. Earlier, they had seemed less than a mile or two away. But the clear desert air made distances deceptive, and he guessed it was all of twelve miles to the High Life.

He mounted the palomino and headed into the teeth of the wind.

Smith ceased fiddling with the wire as soon as he heard Jeff leave. He walked to the door and looked after the rider until he was sure Jeff had not turned back to town; then he ran back to his desk, snatched up the message Jeff had penciled and tucked it carefully into his pocket. There was a greedy look in his eyes as he went out, carefully locking the door behind him.

The mule protested at leaving the comfort of the *ramada,* but Smith never went anywhere without riding that mule. Clutching his top-hat, he started for Jericho.

He was within sight of the Comanche Bar when Tol Oliver intercepted him. The gunman cut his mount across the mule's path, forcing Smith to pull up.

"Where you going, Wireless?"

Smith eyed the man. He wasn't about to shake anything with Oliver.

"My business," he snapped. He tried to ease his animal around Oliver's mount, but stopped, quick

114

panic exploding silently in his eyes as Oliver drew his Colt and rested the muzzle on the pommel in front of him. It was pointing directly at Smith's stomach.

"Now ain't that a coincidence!" Oliver said. His voice seemed pleasant enough, but it had a false ring to it. "I was just on my way to your shack to send a message."

Smith's eyes shuttled from Oliver to the Comanche Bar. He was sure he could find Howard Pope or Frank Connors there.

"I've got a message for Mr. Pope," he lied. "It's important. . . ."

He had expected to pick up drinking money for a month at least from Pope when he brought him the wire.

"Well, now, let me see it," Oliver said. "No use bothering a big man like Mr. Pope with small things, eh, Wireless?"

Smith hesitated. Casually, Oliver's thumb pulled back on the hammer, cocking the pistol. His voice was low and deadly. "Is it, Wireless?"

Reluctantly, Smith handed Jeff's wire to Oliver. "Oughta be worth twenty dollars to Mr. Pope," he whined.

Oliver read the message, his bland face showing no reaction. "Maybe more," he agreed. He made a slight motion with his Colt. "Against the law to hold up a message, ain't it, Wireless?" At Smith's blank look: "Let's send it on to Mr. Sturvesant."

Smith stared. "Maybe Mr. Pope wouldn't—"

"*Mister* Pope just sent me to see you," Oliver interrupted gravely. "He knew about the message."

"Oh. . . ." Smith nodded, but he was two steps behind in his thinking. Then, "You gonna send a fake message?"

Oliver nodded. "You guessed it, Wireless."

They rode on together to the telegraph shack and dismounted. Smith unlocked the door, and they went inside.

Smith settled in his chair and looked at Oliver expectantly, his hand on the key. "What'll I send?"

"This," Oliver replied. He shot Smith twice, although once would have been enough. Smith fell sideways out of his chair, a surprised look in his eyes.

Oliver crossed to the desk and ripped the sender and receiver apparatus from their base and hurled them across the room. Then he carefully went through the small stack of old telegrams filed on a spindle to make sure no copy of Jeff's wire had been made and kept by Smith. He even checked the old wooden file to be certain.

Then he went out, closing the door behind him. The wind singing against the copper strand above him drew his attention. He took out his Colt, fired at the insulator and missed the first shot, irritating him. His next two shots brought the wire down, and he ripped a length of it free and threw it away.

Satisfied no messages would be leaving Jericho for a long time, he mounted and rode away from the shack.

He knew where Jeff Carter was going, because Frank Connors had told him. And Howard Pope had offered quite a bonus for the interfering stranger who had humbled Quincey and killed the Faraday Kid.

He chuckled grimly. He was nowhere near the gun-fighter that Quincey was, or the Kid had been, but he had one thing in his favor. He didn't have their pride, either.

He was going to kill Jeff Carter any way he could—preferably from the back!

THIRTEEN

AMBUSH

THE HIGH LIFE MINE WAS A GASH IN THE SIDE OF THE brown ridge bared to the weltering sun. The original developers had built a ten-by-twenty shed in the hot, mesquite-choked draw below it, and during the flush of their initial haul, when the mine had promised more than it eventually produced, they had laid a narrow-gauge steel track from the shaft down the side of the ridge to the rough wagon road which terminated in the draw by the shed. Small ore cars ran from the mine down to the road and were mule-winched both ways.

The High Life had lasted longer than the other half-dozen hopeful shafts sunk into the long ridge the early miners had named Goldback. But eventually it, like the others, had petered out and its equipment had been left to the weather.

Despite the fact that Howard Pope claimed to have mined more than a quarter of a million dollars in gold from it, he had done little to modernize or renovate the old equipment.

This afternoon the ridge baked in the sun, a drowsy stillness flooding the draw below it. One of Pope's mine guards was sitting back under the shade of a tool shed less than twenty feet from the mine entrance. He was a long splinter of a man, as dark as burnt rawhide. He had a Winchester across his knees, and he was chewing idly on a piece of dried grass.

Turkey Lamont, one of the old Petersen gang, was growing tired of inactivity. He could see little reason for sitting there, guarding a worthless mine—a hole dug into the side of a hot hill.

His partner, Lefty Stevens, had finally decided there was no reason for both of them to sit and sweat it out. Lefty had tossed to see who would ride into town for a bottle, and Lefty had won.

Turkey spat out bits of grass. Thoughts of the bottle Lefty was bringing made his mouth feel as though it were stuffed with cotton. He shifted for a better look down the grown-over wagon road along which Lefty would soon be riding.

He heard the ring of a shod hoof against rock, clear in the stillness. Lamont went tense. He came to his feet, his eyes searching along the draw to the left, then back to the road. A sharp grunt escaped him.

A horse had come into view from the south side of the road. It turned and headed slowly for the sagging tool shed—a magnificent animal, a palomino stallion, still saddled, reins dragging. It was not Lefty's horse!

Turkey Lamont's eyes narrowed with sudden cupidity. He edged forward, rifle ready, his eyes searching the draw for signs of the stallion's rider. The graceful palomino had come to a stop in front of the shed. There was no other sound in the hot stillness of the afternoon.

Turkey's greed got the better of him. He started down the slope towards the road. Whoever had been riding the palomino had probably been thrown. His lips twisted with predatory anticipation. Once he got his hands on that animal—

The palomino edged away from him as he came up, dragging its reins. Turkey shifted his rifle to the crook of his left arm.

"Easy, boy," he muttered. He came closer, intent now on the evasive stallion, and he didn't see the tall man who came out on the road and started at a silent run towards him.

He reached for the animal's trailing reins, caught them, and the stallion jerked his head away, pulling Turkey off balance. He floundered forward, dropping his rifle.

Rage suddenly replaced his cupidity. He scooped up his Winchester, levered a shell into place and swung the muzzle up to target the skittish palomino.

Jeff's sharp voice lashed out from behind him. "You're facing the wrong way, Lamont!"

Turkey whirled and fired and fell, all in one continuous motion. He was dead before he hit the gravel road.

Jeff peered at him through the thinning gunsmoke, his eyes narrow slits of gray. "You had it coming a long time, Turkey!"

He waited, tense and watchful, remembering that the banker, Chandler, had mentioned that Pope kept two men on constant guard. He had made a careful survey before using the palomino as a lure, and he had seen no signs of the second man. He could be waiting inside the mine.

But as the silence lengthened in the hot draw, he

knew he had to take the chance. He led the trained stallion into the draw and tied him in the shade of a clump of cottonwoods. The animal would be out of sight of anyone coming up the road from town.

He paused in the entrance to the mine to take one last look down the road—and he was glad he did.

A rider had appeared on the road below. The man was holding a whisky bottle in his right hand, and he was unsteady in the saddle.

Jeff hesitated. It could be one of the gang coming up to visit Turkey, or the second guard, gone to town for a bottle.

He pulled back within the mine entrance and slid his Colt into his palm. If there was someone waiting in the mine, he reflected coldly, it left him caught somewhere in the middle!

Up on the slope above the draw, Tol Oliver hunkered, rifle across his knees. He had spotted Lefty riding ahead of him half-way to the mine, and at first had been about to join him. Now he was grimly thankful he had changed his mind.

A cautious man who played long odds, Tol knew the explosive capabilities of the man he had come to kill. Jeff would be looking for Turkey and Lefty. He would not be expecting Tol.

He had cut wide of the road and run his horse, wanting to beat Lefty to the mine. He was picketing his horse in a pocket out of sight of the High Life when he heard the shots that killed Turkey. He moved cautiously then, finally gaining the slope and a view of the mine entrance, only to see Jeff Carter step inside and out of rifle range.

His glance moved on to Lefty coming up the road, and a thin smile glinted in Tol's eyes. He didn't give a hoot about Lefty. One less to figure in the cut. He levered a shell into place and waited.

Lefty came riding towards the mine, his gaze swinging towards the tool shed where he expected Turkey to be waiting for him. His voice rang thick and excited in the heavy silence.

"Come on outa the shade, Turkey!" he yelled. "I got news for you."

Jeff waited. He could see Lefty quite well and easily could have killed him without exposing himself.

If there was another guard inside the mine, Lefty's voice should bring him out. If there wasn't—

Lefty pulled up thirty feet from the mine entrance, a sense of foreboding gripping him.

"Turkey!" he called. "Man, this is no time for games!"

Jeff stepped out to the mine entrance. "I've got news for you, Lefty," he said grimly. "Turkey's dead!"

Lefty dropped the bottle. He drew and fired at the figure he remembered vaguely from a previous encounter, and his motions were backed by a desperation that sobered him instantly.

He didn't live long enough to realize anything more. Jeff's two bullets knocked him out of the saddle.

Up on the slope, Oliver's rifle centered on Jeff. From his angle he could see only a partial target. He waited for Jeff to cross out into the open for Lefty's body.

But Jeff didn't move. Tol waited, small beads of sweat gathering on his forehead. His position was cramped now, unbearable, and he shifted slightly, ready to risk a shot at the man in the mine entrance anyhow.

His movement dislodged a small rock on the slope. It rolled down perhaps twenty feet before coming to a spot against a spiny cactus.

Oliver cursed. Below him, Jeff glanced upward towards the sound. But Oliver was down out of sight, screened behind a mesquite bush.

After a moment Jeff turned and ducked into the mine. Oliver's fingers loosened on his rifle.

"Go ahead," he muttered grimly. "Take a look around. I know what you'll find. But you won't live to tell it to anybody. . . ."

He settled back to wait.

As far as he knew, there was only one entrance and one exit to the High Life.

Jeff Carter moved back into the main tunnel and paused to reload his Colt. So far he had been lucky. But he had a gambler's instinct for odds, and he knew, with grim fatalism, that the cards of chance always turned.

Back of his thoughts, the echo of that sliding stone on the slope across the mine entrance bothered him. It could have been a rabbit or a lizard—or a man with a rifle.

A cold sweat chilled his back. He couldn't wait there to find out. He had come there to make sure that Howard Pope's new gold strike was a myth, as Perry Keight had suspected. He could let the U.S. marshal whom John Sturvesant would be sending to Jericho take over from here.

Jeff was no mining engineer, but it did not take him long to assure himself that Pope had been pulling a gigantic swindle. Nowhere in the main shaft nor in the several branching tunnels did he even find evidence of new working.

He was about to step out into the slanting sunlight when the memory of the sliding rock stopped him. He had nothing to go on, really, except a vague and undefinable feeling of danger. But he was a man who had always played his hunches.

He could see Stevens' body lying face down in the sunlight. His horse had wandered off somewhere.

Jeff flattened himself against the side of the entrance and studied what he could see of the opposite slope. There were enough rocks and brush to hide any ambusher.

He speculated briefly on the advisability of waiting until nightfall. Under cover of darkness, it would be easier to make a break, if in truth there was a man waiting out there.

But a hard impatience rode him. He drew his Colt and cocked it. The ambusher would be targeting the entrance in his sights, but he would be expecting Jeff to walk out.

Jeff eased back, judged the angle of the slope and

guessed where the ambusher might be. If there was no one out there, he'd look like a fool, charging out—but only he would know it.

He put everything he had in that sprint out of the mine. And he caught Tol Oliver by surprise. Tol fired hastily and prematurely. He saw his bullet chip splinters from the timber bracing the mine shaft entrance. He saw Jeff swerve towards him, Colt coming up, and he fired again, bitterly fighting the panic rising in him.

Jeff's first shot smashed the bone in his left arm. The rifle slid from Tol's grasp as he lurched up and made a desperate grab for his holster gun.

Jeff killed him before it cleared leather.

The man from Wells Fargo walked the rest of the way up the slope to stand briefly over Oliver's body. He recognized the man as one of the four who had killed Topah's father and mother, and he wasn't sorry he was dead.

He found Lefty Stevens' horse in the draw, its reins tangled in the brush, and he released it, stripping the animal of saddle and blanket. A man who loved horses, he couldn't leave it to die there. He mounted his palomino and went looking for Oliver's horse and turned it loose. He sat in the saddle then, feeling reaction from the shock of the afternoon. He had been lucky all the way.

The palomino under him snorted restlessly. Jeff grinned. "Time we picked up Bill Hayes and got back to town to make Howard Pope and Frank Connors fill in the details."

FOURTEEN

BAD LUCK AT PETE'S SHACK

BILL HAYES SHOT A SWIFT GLANCE THROUGH THE OPEN door of the shack, and for the twentieth time that day he looked down the same angle of trail that led out of the box canyon. It was late, and the sun had gone down behind the canyon walls, and the stillness and the long waiting oppressed him.

The waiting—and the man watching him; watching his every move, from the bunk against the wall.

Bill's wrist ached from the weight of Bart's Colt. It was not a familiar object in his hand. But he had made a mistake early that morning. He had let the marshal talk him into untying him for purposes necessary to hygiene.

Then Bill had found himself faced with a dilemma. As long as he held Bart's gun in his hand, he could keep the bigger man at bay—could force him to do his bidding. But he could not retie the marshal. To attempt it meant getting close to the man, and he could think of no way he could effectively bind Bart without relinquishing, however momentarily, the heavy weapon which gave him the advantage.

He could have forced Bart to turn away and then have cold-bloodedly used the Colt to knock him senseless. But Bill Hayes couldn't bring himself to do it.

So he waited through the long day, waited for Jeff Carter to rescue him from a predicament which was slowly growing unbearable.

In Pete's small corral, the bay which had brought him there stamped restlessly, whinnying with hunger. Bill's glance shifted to the saddle which lay at his feet and the rifle propped against the wall door. He faced around to watch the marshal, and Bart grinned through battered lips, relishing the boy's predicament.

"Waiting getting yuh down, huh?"

Bill made no reply. The marshal shifted slowly, bringing his weight to the edge of the cot. The light in the windowless room was going. It would soon be dark.

"You're a danged fool!" he said flatly. "He'll never show up. Quincey's probably settled with him now."

"If Quincey's tried it, he's probably being fitted for a coffin!" Bill burst out. The words came out of him, but he wasn't that sure.

Why *didn't* Jeff show up?

He was worried about Ellen Bendore. He wanted to be with her, to reassure her. She was alone in Jericho. And he knew how Quincey felt about her.

A helpless anger shook him. He was wasting time. He couldn't go on like this through the night, playing this cat-and-mouse game and feeling at times he was the mouse and the bigger man the cat.

Bart seemed to sense his thoughts. "You got a horse, kid. If you had sense, you'd saddle up and ride out of here. I can't stop you."

The sound of an approaching rider penetrated

slowly into Bill's indecision. Bart had stopped talking, his body tensing, and it was this fact as much as the sound of the rider coming towards the shack which suddenly burst in on him.

Relief flooded through Bill's taut muscles, and he forgot Bart as he turned, stepped through the doorway to hail the rider.

He heard Bart leave the cot, and belatedly he turned back. He fired hastily and missed, and then Bart's heavy shoulder rammed into his mid-section, slamming him against the wall, doubling him in a fall over his gun.

The marshal wasted no time looking for his Colt. He scooped up the rifle and stepped through the doorway in time to see Jeff Carter pull up fifty yards away.

He brought the rifle up and fired, and Jeff tilted sharply and fell out of the saddle.

Bart ran forward, jacking another shell into the rifle chamber, but the palomino was now between him and Jeff's motionless figure. He caught at the stallion's trailing reins just as Bill appeared groggily in the doorway behind him and fired a shot which did not even come close.

But it served to direct Bart's attention to immediate flight. He jerked the palomino around and stepped into the saddle, and in the next moment he had to fight desperately to stay seated as the big stallion tried to shake him off.

When the flurry subsided, the marshal was still in the saddle and already far down the trail. The shadows were blurring details in the box canyon.

He dragged in a deep breath of relief and looked back. The corral was between him and the shack, but he could see the bay nosing the top rail—and beyond he saw Bill Hayes kneeling beside the Wells Fargo man's limp figure.

A wave of exultation surged through the town marshal. What other men, swaggering gunmen like Quincey, had tried to do, he had done with one swift rifle shot!

He could probably finish off the Hayes kid, too. But if Bill holed up in the shack, it might be a long job. He saw the bay move against the corral bars again, and solution thinned his battered lips.

Sighting carefully, he sent a slug smashing into the bay's head.

He saw the animal go down, and then he had a glimpse of young Hayes standing clear of Jeff's body, and he jerked his rifle muzzle up again. But the mincing palomino spoiled his shot, and his next try clicked on an empty chamber.

Cursing, Bart tossed the now useless (to him) rifle aside and turned the palomino towards the trail out of the canyon. Behind him he heard a Colt smash against the stillness, but the bullet hit nowhere near him.

The marshal fought the big palomino most of the way across a corner of the Sinks. The horse was tricky, but Bart hung on, forcing the animal eventually to a steady, loping gait.

The stars came out in a blue-black sky. It was late that night when he neared the dry river bed which separated Jericho from the Sinks. He turned the palomino along the bank and headed for the plank bridge a quarter of a mile away.

The lights of the town lulled him. He settled back, a grin widening his mouth as he anticipated the reaction of his companions when he told them that he had killed Jeff Carter.

Ten yards from the bridge, the palomino exploded into violence. The big stallion went straight into the air as if he wanted to paw at the stars, and Bart was shaken loose. He fell in a crouch and started up as the animal whirled on him. The impact of the horse's shoulder sent him reeling. The lawman recovered, only to see the stallion come at him, rear up to strike at him with deadly hoofs.

Bart lunged sideways and dived headlong into the *arroyo*. He rolled and crashed through the brush and staggered to his feet, half-expecting the big stallion to come down after him.

But the palomino halted at the edge of the dry wash. For a moment he was outlined against the stars—a magnificent animal in silhouette. Then he turned, whinnied to the night wind and started at a trot towards the dark hills.

Bart scrambled up the opposite bank and watched the horse fade into the night. If he had had a gun he would have used it to kill the palomino. He vented his rage in a shake of his fist.

"You red devil!" he snarled. "Go on back to him! But he'll never ride you again, you danged outlaw!"

Howard Pope was in the Comanche Bar, seated at a

table by himself with a bottle and a glass before him, when Bart pushed through the door and made his way to him.

Curious eyes followed the town marshal's progress, noting his blood-smeared face, his torn and soiled clothes, his empty holster. He ignored the stares. Reaching Pope's table, he pulled out a chair and sagged into it and immediately reached for the bottle. He used the scarred man's glass and poured himself a stiff drink which he slopped over the rim. Some of it dribbled down his chin as he lifted the glass to his lips.

Placing the glass down, he reached for the bottle and was starting to fill it again when Pope's fingers closed around his wrist.

"Where the devil have *you* been?" Pope's voice was a harsh whisper.

Whitey Smith and a lanky, sad-faced man named Peebles were standing at the end of the long bar with two of the house entertainers. They quit chatting when Bart came in and drifted over to Pope's table.

Bart kept his fingers around the half-filled whisky glass. "I need another drink," he growled.

Pope scowled, his scar tissue wrinkling under his glittering eyes. "Where's young Hayes?"

"Marooned in the hills," Bart answered. His voice was low. He didn't want it to carry beyond the table. "I left him at Injun Pete's shack."

He pulled the bottle to him and started to pour as Pope snarled, "You left him there—*alive?*"

Bart shrugged. "Yeah." He filled the glass and tossed the liquor down and wiped his mouth with the back of his hand. He heard Whitey snicker. His shoulders stiffened, and he half-rose from his chair, an ugly rage darkening his battered face.

Pope said, "Sit down, Bart." His voice held an icy expectancy.

Bart said grimly, "I've had a rough time, Pope. Let me tell it my way." He looked up at Peebles and Whitey, and both men grinned sheepishly.

Whitey said, "Sorry about sounding off, Bart. You look like a hoss kicked you around a bit."

Pope pushed his chair back and stood up. Too many men were watching them. "We'll use one of the back rooms," he decided. "Whitey, bring another bottle and some glasses from the bar."

They listened to Bart's story in the privacy of the back room. At the finish of it, Pope said, "You sure you killed him?"

He didn't sound convinced. He was remembering the easy assurance with which the Faraday Kid had promised to dispose of the meddlesome Wells Fargo man. But it was Monty and the Kid who were lying in pine boxes in the local undertaker's back room.

Bart hesitated and covered his hesitation by reaching for the whisky bottle. "Sure," he lied. "I made sure of him before I left. I would have gotten the Hayes kid, too, but I ran out of rifle shells."

Whitey cut in dryly, "Quincey won't thank you for it, Bart. I never saw him want to kill a man as bad as he wants to kill that Wells Fargo investigator."

Bart sneered. "Where is Quincey?"

"Sleeping off a drunk—and a busted jaw," Peebles

132

answered for Whitey. "I saw him in Baldy's back room a couple of hours ago."

Whitey turned at a knock on the back-room door, then glanced at Pope. Pope nodded. Whitey opened the door. Frank Connors came inside, holding a long white envelope in his hand. He saw Bart and stopped.

"When did you get back?"

"A few minutes ago," Bart answered sourly.

Connors glanced around the room. "I didn't see Tol up front. Didn't he get back yet?"

Pope frowned. He had forgotten Oliver. But Whitey, Tol's sidekick, hadn't.

Whitey said, "Didn't he go up to the mine?"

Connors looked at Pope. We sent him to check on that telegram Carter was sending. Might be he went after Carter on his own."

"I don't care where he went!" Pope snarled. He was eyeing the envelope in Pope's hand. "You check the late stage?"

Connors nodded. He stepped up and dropped the envelope on the table in front of the mine owner, and then, reading the grim urgency in the crippled man's eyes, he tore the envelope open for him. The others crowded around as Pope separated the bank draft from the Wells Fargo letter accompanying it.

Howard Pope started to laugh. "In full payment of your loss," he read. Then he crumpled the letter in his fist and discarded it.

"We're through waiting, boys. I said we'd clear it big, didn't I?" His voice rang with shrill triumph. "A quarter of a million from Wells Fargo, and that much in gold waiting to be picked up in the canyon!"

Whitey's tone was awed. "A half-million American pesos! I'm taking my share and heading for Mexico."

Connors interrupted him. "I'll take my cut, too, Howard, right after Chandler cashes this draft for us. I've got plans, too."

Pope's eyes glittered. "What sort of plans, Frank?"

The tall man shrugged. "I promised a woman I'd take her back to New Orleans." He hesitated, trying to gauge the red glitter in Pope's eyes. "You won't be needing me around any more."

Pope shook his head. "This is the split-up," he agreed. "Let's drink on it, boys."

Connors remained for one round, then left.

Pope watched the door close behind him. "Blasted ladies' man!" he sneered. But inside himself he felt the old gnawing sickness, and a latent envy inspired his brief comment:

"I never did *need* him around. . . ."

FIFTEEN

TOPAH TAKES A HAND

Bill Hayes squatted on his heels and heaved a sigh of relief as Jeff groaned softly and moved his head. He had dragged the limp Wells Fargo man into the shack, out of the chill, and stood beside him as the sun went down and darkness settled like a smothering blanket in the box canyon.

Bart's snap shot had furrowed a deep gash just over Jeff's left ear. Bill had washed and bandaged it as well as he could, but, as Jeff had remained unconscious through the hours, fear had gripped him.

He cursed himself for giving Bart his break. But after a while he quit berating himself and ventured out to look the situation over.

The bay horse was dead in the corral. If Pete had kept any stock in the small enclosure, it had been run off or had strayed.

He had considered the long walk across the Sinks to Jericho, but he knew he could not leave until he found out about Jeff. He couldn't leave this man unattended.

Now, with a candle he had found in a cupboard flickering on a shelf behind him, he saw Jeff's eyes open and look at him without focus.

Thank God, he breathed to himself; and then, audibly: "How are you?"

He saw Jeff's eyes finally focus, and a small smile struggled to Jeff's lips.

"I'm alive," Jeff said. "I guess that's good enough."

He swung his legs over the side of the cot and sat up, then suddenly buried his face in his hands as nausea threatened to black him out.

Bill Hayes said quickly: "I'll get you some water," and turned to the water bucket in a corner.

"A shot of whisky would be better," Jeff said, hurting. Then, as Bill stopped, cup in hand, he grinned weakly. "But water will do fine."

He drank just enough to moisten his mouth, spat it out, then drank the next swallows down. Then, feeling a little better, he reached up and probed gently with his fingers at the bandage around his head wound.

"What happened?"

Bill shamefacedly told him. "I should have killed him, I guess, when I had the chance. But I couldn't."

"Just as well," Jeff said. "Killing can get to be a habit." His eyes shadowed, and he looked off towards the open door where starshine lightened the canyon. "I was sort of getting back into it myself."

He took a deep breath and stood up. "It's better outside," he said, and walked to the door. His head began to pound, and he leaned against the framing, looking towards the corral.

Bill, coming up behind him, said: "We're stuck here, Jeff. Bart took your horse and killed the bay." His voice was bitter.

Jeff didn't say anything. The night air felt good in his lungs. His head began to clear, leaving him only

136

the pain of the gash to live with.

He went back into the cabin. "We'll rest up for a while," he said. "Then we'll start walking." He sat down on the edge of his cot. "You remember any small ranch hereabouts where we might pick up a couple of mounts?"

Bill shook his head. "The ranches are all south of the Sinks."

He paused, turning towards the door. Jeff eyed him. "Thought I heard something," Bill muttered. Then, sharply, "Someone's out there!"

Jeff came off the cot, his Colt in his hand. He blew out the candle in one puff and flattened against the wall next to the door. Bill remained rooted where he was standing.

Outside, the shadows were deceiving in the starlight. The wind played tricks in the cottonwoods. Jeff waited tensely, his eyes searching the shadows.

A horse whinnied. The sound was at once familiar and a warning to Jeff. He whistled back. There was a crashing in the brush off the trail, and then the palomino came into view, reins dragging, saddle slightly tilted.

Jeff breathed a sigh of relief. He turned to Bill Hayes who now joined him in the doorway.

"Reckon we've got our transportation," he said. He looked up at the stars. "We'll give him a breather, then go in. We should make Jericho by morning."

The early-morning sun slanted its warm rays over the flat roof of the Overland Stage office. From the middle window of Frank Hayes' living-room Topah watched the town awaken.

The narrow-shouldered bank teller opened the bank door and went inside. He raised the shades in the windows fronting the street and went behind the barrier to his cage to begin the day's work.

Calvin Chandler arrived a few minutes later, nodded good morning to the teller and disappeared inside his office.

The teller counted his money twice and checked yesterday's entries. He had given in to his loneliness last night and frequented one of the bawdy houses, and this morning he was sick of himself and had a headache to boot.

He looked through the bars of his cage as Ellen Bendore came in. The girl looked tired; she looked ten years older than she was.

She said: "Is Mr. Chandler in?"

The teller nodded and indicated the closed door. He watched her push through the railing gate and disappear inside Chandler's office. He knew she had more troubles than he had, but it did not serve to brighten his day. He started to sort out the bills in front of him.

Five minutes after Ellen Bendore's entrance, seven men rode up to the bank. Three of them dismounted and went inside. Four remained mounted and waiting at the tie-rack.

Chandler was trying to reassure Ellen concerning Bill Hayes and Jeff Carter when the teller came to the door of his office.

"Mr. Pope wants to see you, sir."

Chandler frowned. He went to the door and regarded the three men standing in front of the teller's cage. A premonition of trouble sent a warning through him. Behind Pope's scarred face he could see Frank Connors and Quincey.

"Better wait in here," he told Ellen. "I'll join you in a few minutes."

But Ellen remained in the doorway, staring at the waiting men.

Chandler went out to join Pope by the teller's window. The mine owner handed him the Wells Fargo bank draft, grinning crookedly. "I want to cash this in," he said peremptorily.

Chandler glanced at the amount and shook his head. "I don't have that much money in the safe, Howard. If you'll give me a few days—"

"We'll take what you have—all of it!" Quincey snapped. His jaw was still badly swollen and discolored, but it no longer pained him as much as it had.

The banker squared his shoulders, his eyes meeting the gunman's sneering gaze. "Pope," he said sharply, "you cashing this draft, or trying to rob my bank?"

"The draft's good, isn't it, Chandler?"

Chandler nodded. He didn't like the way Quincey was eyeing Ellen.

"Then cash it!" Pope rasped.

"I told you I haven't that much money."

Frank Connors interrupted him. "We'll take what you have on hand, Calvin. You can credit the rest to Pope's account."

Pope glared at Connors, but refrained from countermanding his mine superintendent. "All right," he said to the banker. "Let's see what you have."

Chandler glanced at Quincey, whose hand was resting on his gun butt. He shrugged. "Open the safe, Harry," he instructed his teller. He reached in under the grille and handed the teller's pen to Pope. "Endorse it, Howard."

Pope scratched his name on the back of the bank draft, and Chandler pushed it under the grille. Harry was standing in front of the open safe, looking back to Chandler for instructions.

"Put it in one of the bank's canvas bags," Chandler said. "We'll check the count with Mr. Pope." His voice was grim. "You're forcing me into a bad position, Howard," he pointed out. "Until I get credit on this draft, I'll have to close the bank."

Pope laughed shortly. "My business has been closed for three months," he reminded Chandler.

Chandler's lips tightened. "I don't have to do this—" he began, but broke off as Quincey edged towards him.

Harry lifted a stuffed canvas bag to the teller's window and pushed it towards Pope. "One hundred and eighty-seven thousand dollars," he said. His voice was trembling.

Pope's fingers closed eagerly over the bag. "We'll take your teller's count, Chandler." He started away from the window towards the door.

It opened, and Dolores Bendore marched in. She wore a duster over her suit, and she was carrying a handbag. Ellen had come to stand just inside the railing, but Dolores did not even glance at her step-daughter.

She brushed past the mine owner and caught Frank Connors by the arm. "Frank!" Her voice was shrill. There was anger in it, and a measure of panic, too. "You were planning to leave without me! I saw you ride by—"

Quincey whirled and backhanded her across the mouth. It was a vicious blow; it split her lips and sent her reeling against the railing, where she slumped in a dazed, moaning heap.

Connors whirled on the gunslinger, his action instinctive. "Damn you, Quincey!" His open hand cuffed the gunman across the face.

Pain shot through Quincey's head, momentarily crazing him. His gun hand came up, and his shot spun Connors around. Frank fell against the cage, caught at the small bars with his left hand and tried to reach his small-caliber under-arm gun with his right. Quincey's second shot loosened his grip; he sagged limply to the floor.

As if Quincey's shots were a signal, a rifle opened up from Hayes' office across the street.

Pope ran to the door and looked out. There appeared to be a pitched battle going on between the four mounted men at the bank rail and a hidden rifleman in the office across the street.

"Bart!" he called sharply. "Bring three horses around to the back!"

Bart was momentarily engaged in firing at the window over the Overland Stage office and didn't

141

hear him. "For God's sake, Bart—hurry!"

Bart whirled to obey. Pope ducked back inside the bank and crossed to where Dolores was slowly getting to her feet. She looked down at Frank Connors, horror in her eyes.

"Frank!" she whispered. "Frank, I didn't mean to."

Pope grabbed her arm, hurting her as he forced her towards the back door. She balked then, turning. He shoved a shoulder gun against her ribs.

"You've got a choice," he rasped. "You can die here with him—or you can come with me!"

The flaming hatred in Pope's eyes shocked her. Numbly she let herself be pushed out through the back door.

The outbreak of violence had stunned Chandler. He made no effort to stop Pope. But Ellen's sudden cry of pain as Quincey jerked her towards the door with him caused him to lunge at the gunman.

Quincey whirled and clubbed at the banker with his Colt. Chandler reeled back, blood streaming from a gash on his head.

Quincey kept the girl in front of him, using her as a shield as he went down the bank steps to his horse.

Only two men were still mounted, firing desperately at all the windows of the stage office across the street. Whitey Smith lay sprawled under the tie-rack, and as Quincey went by him he had the inconsequential thought that Whitey would never make it to Mexico now.

He glanced around for Bart, but the marshal was nowhere in sight. Derek, a big, powerful man, and

Peebles were fighting their frightened horses.

Peebles yelled: "What happened in there, Quincey? Where's Pope?"

Quincey didn't answer him. He turned to Derek. "Help me get her up!" he snapped. He was standing beside his rangy chestnut.

Derek rode up and reached for Ellen. She offered no resistance. She seemed shocked beyond all movement.

Derek hoisted her up to the chestnut's saddle, and Quincey got up behind her. He pulled away from the rail.

"Let's get out of here!" he yelled to Peebles and Derek.

Derek started to turn his mount; he grunted as the rifle slug tore through him, spilling him out of the saddle. Quincey turned and fired hastily at a blurred face he glimpsed in the shattered window above the stage office.

"Topah!" He swore in surprise.

Peebles was already far up the street. Quincey raked his mount with his spurs, and the chestnut lunged ahead.

The rifle shot hit him between the shoulder-blades, flattened against a rib and tore him from the saddle. He fell loosely, rolling a few feet in the dust of the street. The chestnut kept running, with Ellen clinging to him, her fingers twisted in the animal's mane. But she was no rider. At the end of the street she slipped off. She landed on her feet, off balance. She fell forward, and the impact left her momentarily stunned.

Behind the windows of the stage office, Topah leaned stoically on the muzzle of his Henry and stared at the bodies in front of the bank. There was a cut on his cheek, caused by flying glass.

He saw men emerge cautiously from doorways. Some of them started for the bank. Topah didn't move. Not even when the palomino carrying Bill Hayes and Jeff Carter came at a weary trot into town did he move.

Topah was thinking back to his mother and father, and two lonely graves in a small box canyon. . . .

SIXTEEN

THE QUICKSAND WAY

JEFF CARTER PULLED THE WEARY PALOMINO TO A STOP in front of the bank. A small cluster of men stood around the body of Quincey fifty feet up the street. Some of them were glancing towards the shattered windows of the Overland Stage office.

The bodies of Derek and Whitey lay where they had fallen. Jeff slid out of the saddle and turned to the bank just as Chandler staggered into view. The banker seemed dazed. Blood caked the side of his face.

He stared at the scene in front of his bank, and then he saw Jeff and Bill and a sigh escaped him. "You came a little late."

He started down the steps towards them and stumbled. Jeff caught him before he fell.

Chandler looked up into Bill's white face. "Ellen. . . . Quincey took her with him!"

Bill stiffened. Jeff frowned. "Quincey's dead," he said.

Behind him, Ellen's voice rang out, sobbing: "Bill—oh, Bill—"

Young Hayes turned. Ellen was coming towards him, her face dusty. He ran to her, a great gladness in his eyes. "Ellen, Ellen, you all right?"

She nodded, and he gathered her into his arms, oblivious to the onlookers.

Chandler heaved a sigh of relief. "Thank God she's safe."

"What happened?" Jeff's voice was grim.

"Pope"—it was an effort for Chandler to talk—"came in to cash his Wells Fargo insurance draft. Was in a hurry. I gave him everything I had in the safe."

The small group clustered around Quincey's body dissolved. Some of them came towards the bank.

Chandler's pained gaze steadied on the nearest man, a clerk in Parker's Mercantile Store.

"George, get Doctor Haywood here right away!"

George hesitated, then turned and began to run up the street. Chandler looked at Jeff.

"Frank Connors—inside. Quincey shot him. But I think he's still alive."

They went into the bank, a small group of silent, bewildered townspeople following.

Connors lay on his back, blood making a mess of his white shirt front. His breathing was shallow, faint. But his eyes were open, and he recognized Jeff as the Wells Fargo man and Chandler bent over him.

"Bart said you were dead. . . ." A pained smile twisted across his lips. "Guess you're a hard man to kill. . . ."

"He's dead," Chandler told him. "Ellen is safe."

Connors wet his lips. "Dolores—?"

Jeff swung his attention to the banker. "Dolores?" he repeated. "Was she here?"

The banker nodded. "Pope took her with him."

Connors' weak voice swung Jeff's attention back to him. "She was coming with me—New Orleans—"

146

His eyes held a mocking light. "No woman for a horse ranch, Jeff. Not Dolores. Bright lights, gay parties—I had the money to give it all to her."

He coughed sharply, and now a trickle of blood showed at the corner of his mouth. He was dying, and Connors knew it.

"Damn Pope," he said bitterly.

Jeff took in a deep breath. "You don't owe Pope anything now. Tell us what happened to Frank Hayes."

Connors eyed him, not saying anything. He didn't like Jeff, but he hated Pope more.

"Why did Pope hate Frank Hayes?"

Connors closed his eyes, as if he wanted to think. His lips moved. "Goes back more than twenty years. Real name is Carey Mason. He, Frank and another man—name of Russ Orlin—prospected the Captains. Morado and his Apaches caught them in Lost Springs Canyon. Pope and Orlin captured. Hayes and Indian guide got away. Pope never forgot—"

He paused, and a great tiredness came over his face. His lungs filled once more in a shuddering gasp, then stilled.

Jeff straightened and looked at Chandler. His face was grim. "I'll need a fresh horse."

Chandler nodded. He looked at Harry, who had not moved from behind the teller's cage. "Get him my black mare."

He walked with Jeff to the door. George and a short, pudgy man, Doctor Haywood, were just coming up.

147

Chandler's voice was tired. "I think he's dead, Doctor. But you better make it official."

Jeff was looking across the street to the stage office. He started as Topah emerged from the alley leading back to the Overland's stables. Topah was riding a pinto horse, the Henry held across his pommel.

There was a quiet dignity in the boy as he rode slowly, with quiet defiance, across the street, turning towards the road out of town.

Jeff crossed in front of him. "Topah, you remember me?"

The boy's face was pinched with fatigue. He studied Jeff for a moment, then nodded.

Jeff said, "I came here to help Frank Hayes. He was a friend of your father."

The boy's eyes told him nothing.

"You know the old Apache way into Lost Springs Canyon, don't you?"

A glint came into Topah's black eyes. "I know the way," he said.

The sun burned down over the Sinks, and a wind stirred along the baked gullies. Bart was falling behind Pope and Dolores. His horse had suffered a stone bruise sliding down a gully and was limping badly.

He felt the animal under him begin to weaken, and a curse welled up in his throat. He had to keep up! He knew Pope. The mine owner, leading Dolores' horse, wouldn't turn a hand to help him!

Bart turned and looked back to the lone rider raising dust behind him. The figure danced in front of his eyes. But it looked as if Peebles had been the only other man to get away.

His horse began to stumble. He slid his rifle free, a plan shaping up in his mind. It was every man for himself now, and forget about Peebles!

He pulled up and dismounted to wait for Peebles. He stood behind his lame horse, his rifle hidden from the approaching rider.

Peebles was mounted on a good horse. He slowed down as he saw Bart. Up ahead, pulling away from them, rode Pope and Dolores.

"Glad you waited for me," Peebles called. "That big hombre you said you killed up in Injun Pete's canyon is behind us, with that Indian kid, Topah—"

Bart's rifle bullet cut him short. He fell forward on his pommel, clutched at it and started to slide down. Bart was already running towards him. Peebles' eyes stared accusingly at the town marshal as he slipped free and fell under the animal's feet.

Bart caught the animal's reins and swung aboard. Peebles rolled over on his side and tried to reach his holstered gun. Tears of frustration came into his eyes, but he didn't have the strength. He moaned softly and went limp.

Jeff and Topah found Peebles still alive. He had a fighting chance if he could make it back to town.

Carter hoisted the desperately wounded man aboard Bart's lamed animal. He pointed the mare towards Jericho.

"Hang on," he told Peebles. He slapped the horse's rump, and he and Topah watched as the mare went into a jog towards town.

They caught up to Bart and Pope and Dolores at the entrance to Lost Springs Canyon. For a quarter of a mile the bogs shimmered in the sun. Behind them, the sharp walls of the canyon loomed dark and forbidding.

Pope and Bart were afoot. Pope was leading Dolores' horse and his own. He was well ahead of Bart, who was slowly picking his way across the treacherous ground, following Pope's footsteps. Dolores lay slumped over her horse's neck. The ride from the bank had been a nightmare.

Bart looked back as Jeff and Topah halted at the edge of the quicksand way. Fear tightened his face. "Pope!" he yelled. "Pope—wait!"

Pope looked back. Shock went through him as he recognized Jeff.

Damn Bart, he thought bitterly.

He dropped the lead rope to Dolores' horse and pressed forward, using his own animal as a shield between him and Jeff and Topah. Left to itself, Dolores' horse stopped, then moved forward uncertainly. Its probing forefoot came down on soft sand, and he drew back, suddenly afraid, and whinnied uneasily.

Dolores roused and looked about her. The hemming walls of the canyon seemed to press down around her. She had a moment of stark terror as she saw Pope up ahead, abandoning her. She screamed!

The animal under her shied off. It stepped out into the shimmering bog that had no bottom and began to flounder.

Five hundred yards behind her, Jeff broke into a run to catch her, but Topah headed him off.

"You follow me!" he said quickly.

Jeff paused. Up ahead, Bart was running, leaving his horse behind. Desperation drove him. Dolores screamed at him as he went by her, but he ignored her.

The quicksand way shimmered ominously in the slanting sunlight. It seemed to ripple and erase Pope's passage. Bart kept his eyes on the mine owner. Up ahead, Pope had gained firm ground and, mounting, was riding into the shadows of the canyon.

Bart yelled: "Pope!" But his call was lost against the towering canyon walls, and came back in a mocking echo.

A bubble formed and broke in the wet sand ahead of him. He swerved wildly and stepped off firm ground into sand that had no footing. Momentum sent him sprawling. He fought wildly, panic driving him. He flailed away at the soft sucking sand like a madman until exhaustion claimed him.

He lay spent, buried to his chin. His eyes turned to the canyon wall, and he uttered one last curse before the yielding, pressing sand engulfed him.

A hundred yards back, Jeff was leading his horse, carefully following Topah. Dolores was clinging to her horse, her face buried in his coarse mane. The frightened animal was weakening. It had floundered

151

around in the treacherous sand, its front legs still on firm ground but its hind legs sinking deeper.

Jeff called: "Dolores!"

The woman roused slowly and looked back. It took a moment for her to recognize Jeff.

"Jeff!" she cried. Then, sobbing, "Oh, Jeff. . . ."

She started to slide from the saddle, but Jeff's voice stopped her. "Don't move until we get there, Dolores!"

She clung to her saddle, sobbing softly. The horse struggled weakly as Jeff and Topah came up. Jeff reached out and pulled Dolores to safety. She clung to him, crying. Slowly Jeff calmed her.

Topah was staring towards the canyon into which Pope had disappeared.

It took Jeff and Topah five minutes to free Dolores' mount, with the aid of a rope and the careful maneuvering of Jeff's horse.

"Wait here," he told her. "I'll be back."

He turned to Topah. "Lead me across to the canyon. Then come back and stay with her."

Dolores clung to him. "No, Jeff, no!" Her eyes were wide with terror.

"I'll come back," he repeated, and motioned to Topah. They moved out across the shimmering bogs, Jeff following close behind the Indian boy, leading his mount.

Dolores sank down on the firm ground beside her tired horse and buried her face in her hands.

Carey Mason, alias Howard Pope, left his cayuse at

152

the bottom of a steep slope, by the ruins of an old stone hut. The bones of a man long dead lay whitening in the sun before the abandoned shack; the bones of a man who once had been his partner—Russ Orlin.

Old memories crowded through Mason's head. Twenty years ago he had been a whole man, a handsome man, a man from whom women would not have turned away.

He stood beside his panting horse, listening to the deep stillness in the canyon. Around him the walls rose, blotting out the sky.

Morado's old hideout! Safe behind a quicksand barrier only Morado's Apaches had known how to cross; and the old cavalry scout, Pete, who had been Frank Hayes' friend.

The walls seemed to crowd the memories in on the scarred man, and he turned to follow with bitter eyes the dim path that led to the hut and up to the ledge where a hole was like an ink blot in the cliff.

They had heard the stories of an old Spanish goldmine in Lost Springs Canyon, and he and Orlin had prevailed on Frank Hayes to have Pete guide them across the quicksand way. Morado and his warriors were away, raiding in Mexico, and would be no trouble.

In the gathering gloom, Mason, alias Pope, laughed bitterly now, and his cayuse moved away from him, dragging its reins.

They had crossed the quicksand moat and entered the canyon and found the ledge and the ancient mine opening, a shaft long abandoned by the Spaniards who had worked it.

But Mason hadn't known that then. He and Russ had wanted to start working it at once. Frank and Pete had drifted back to the canyon entrance—to gather firewood, Frank had said, to make camp.

Mason shrank within himself as memories thronged through him. He and Russ had received no warning. They had emerged from the old mine shaft in time to see a file of warriors ride up to the stone hut.

Mason's left hand came up to touch his scarred cheeks. Russ Orlin had died horribly—but he had died a quick death. He had died a whole man.

It would have been better, he thought, if Morado had killed him then, along with Orlin. But the Apache chief had let him live—broken, scarred. For two years he had been treated worse than a dog in Morado's camp—beaten and stoned by the younger warriors, scorned and spat upon by the squaws.

The scars on his face were less disfiguring than the scars they had carved in his soul.

He had learned later that Frank Hayes and Pete had got away without being seen by Morado's Apaches, and for this he never forgave Frank. He had spent long years searching for his former partner, only eventually to come upon him in Jericho at a time when he had all but given up hope of finding him.

Now he heard the sharp ring of hoofs in the canyon behind him, and Mason was suddenly aware of the present—of the drag of the canvas bag he still clutched in his good hand.

He let his gaze range wildly along the hemming walls, knowing there was no escape—that Lost

Springs Canyon, safe behind its protective moat of quicksand, could also be a trap.

The bend in the canyon hid the rider, but the sound of his coming rang loud in the deep stillness. And Mason knew who the rider was—a tall man who had not believed Frank Hayes had turned outlaw, a man who had relentlessly torn apart all Pope's careful planning.

Fear turned him towards the dim path leading up to the ledge. . . .

A few moments later, Jeff Carter pulled up before the ruins of the stone hut; his gaze moved dispassionately over the bones of Russ Orlin, following the faint trail up to the mine shaft on the ledge.

Mason had disappeared. But the dark mouth of the abandoned mine told him where Mason had gone.

He went up the trail, his Colt drawn, his eyes riveted on the angle of the mine opening. If Mason were inside, he was not tipping his hand.

The silence pressed down on the canyon; it had the hushed quality of a cathedral. The slight movement of the horses waiting below rang sharply in the stillness.

Jeff paused by the mine entrance.

"Mason!" His voice was loud in the quiet. "I'm coming in after you!"

For a long moment there was no answer. Then Mason's laughter rang out—a sobbing, wild sound that raised the hair on Jeff's neck!

"A half-million dollars, Carter!" Mason's voice rang out. "All mine! Mine and Russ Orlin's!" His wild laughter echoed in the canyon. "We paid for it, Russ and I! We burned for it! You hear me, Carter? That's Russ down there—that's his skull leering up at you!"

Jeff edged towards the opening. From inside the mine a .38 pistol barked spitefully, and the slug chipped stone from the timbers framing the shaft.

Mason laughed again. "You listening, Carter? There were three of us a long time ago: Frank Hayes, Russ and me. But Frank let us die, while he went free!"

Jeff set himself. "Where's Frank Hayes now?"

"At the bottom of that quicksand—if there is a bottom to it!" Mason's laughter had a triumphant edge. "I searched for Frank for eighteen years—"

Jeff lunged into the mine. He had closed his eyes before making the move so that the difference in the intensity of light within the tunnel wouldn't be so great.

He lunged aside as Mason's gun sent a spurt of flame in the darkness ahead. He fired twice, the .45's heavier reports shuddering in the ancient tunnel. Somewhere in the mine a small slide started.

Carey Mason was dead when Jeff bent over him. He was slumped over a heavy iron box. A quarter of a million dollars in gold was in that box.

A canvas bank bag lay beside Mason, some of the crisp greenbacks spilling out. Jeff picked up the money and stuffed it back inside the bag. The Wells Fargo strongbox would be safe there until he came back for it.

SEVENTEEN

"GOODBYE, JEFF"

JEFF CARTER SAID GOODBYE TO BILL HAYES AND Ellen Bendore in Ellen's home a few days later. He still wore a bandage over the cut above his eye, but it was a neater job, put there by Doctor Haywood.

"Will you come back for the wedding?" Ellen asked.

Jeff shook his head. "I'll say my congratulations now." He shook Bill Hayes' hand and kissed Ellen lightly on the mouth.

He went up the street and stopped at the bank to see Chandler. The banker waved him to a chair, but Jeff said: "I've got a long ride ahead. I want to get an early start."

"John Sturvesant wired he's coming to Jericho for the wedding." There was a protest in Chandler's voice. "He'll want to see you."

"He knows where he can find me," Jeff said. He dug a twenty-dollar gold piece out of his pocket and placed it on Chandler's desk. "Buy the kids a wedding present for me."

He started to leave, but Chandler said, "Dolores Bendore wants to see you. She's waiting for you across the street."

Jeff hesitated a moment, then nodded. "I'll see her."

From a distance Dolores looked tall and beautiful and untouched by the violence that had shaken Jericho. She was waiting on the porch of the Overland Stage for the coach that was to take her on the first leg of a long journey back to New Orleans.

She turned as Jeff came up, and a smile came into her eyes. She put out a gloved hand to him.

"I'm glad you came, Jeff."

Jeff took it, admiring her poise. "You look beautiful," he said, and meant it, and saw the light of appreciation that flickered in her violet eyes.

"You won't come with me?"

He shook his head.

"Jeff"—her voice was low—"is it because of Frank Connors?"

"No." He considered the matter again, knowing that Connors had been right, and he voiced his opinion. "You'd never be happy on a horse ranch in Red Rock, Dolores. And," he added, "I've lost my taste for cards—and New Orleans."

He started to turn away.

"Jeff—wait." Her voice pulled him around. She put her arms around him and kissed him, and he felt the sadness in her.

"Goodbye, Jeff."

The scent of lilacs lingered a long time, but the ghost that had haunted him faded more with each stride.

The palomino, rested and eager to get going, pawed at the stable floor as Jeff saddled him.

"All right," Jeff said, smiling. "I'll let you run—all

the way back to Red Rock, if you want."

He was thinking of Mady Wilson as he rode out of Jericho—wondering if she would be waiting.

Center Point Publishing
600 Brooks Road ● PO Box 1
Thorndike ME 04986-0001 USA

(207) 568-3717

US & Canada:
1 800 929-9108